REVENANT

**No matter what form they take,
they're coming for you...**

Edited by Dorothy Davies

REVENANT

**No matter what form they take,
they're coming for you…**

GRAVESTONE PRESS

Gravestone Press
is an imprint of
Fiction4All
www.fiction4all.com

This Edition
Published 2022

TABLE OF CONTENTS

Never Too Late To Die

Olivia Arieti

Those were rainy days and Norman detested the rain; that sullen wetness got on his nerves just like his wife's continuous visits.

"You're stone dead, Alyssa, what do you want from me?" he shouted on seeing the spectre plummet into his room.

"Watching you rot would be great, I didn't like your dirty trick at all."

"Get out of here," he pleaded, exhausted.

The tragedy had occurred years ago on a bleak evening exactly like that one. She insisted on spending the weekend at their holiday home by the lake. No cottage cosier than theirs with the garden full of flower beds, willow trees with exceptionally long drooping branches and a private dock where their motor boat waited for them. He loved going there but not when he had to hand in a manuscript to an unforgiving editor and needed to remain in his studio and write till his eyes were red and fingers hurt. Alyssa always had it her way; her insistence was so unnerving that he ended up giving in.

Theirs had been love at first sight, probably too much at first sight for after the second month of marriage, they found out they were totally incompatible. Alyssa was impulsive, whimsical and hated whatever her husband did. Writing was a waste of time, not profitable and most of all it estranged him from her world where shopping sprees, dinner parties and all sort of leisure were predominant. She was a gorgeous lady with enticing eyes and affable manners and flirting was her favourite pastime, despite being married.

Norman never doubted she had cheated on him, but he didn't care much… His work absorbed him completely. It needed tranquillity¹ and even a good dose of solitude. Marrying a woman like Alyssa had been a big mistake.

Luckily, the time spent stabbing the keyboard wasn't as unprofitable as it seemed. One best seller followed the other, two films were made out of them and fame and, most of all, lots of money rolled in. That was when he purchased the cottage.

Never had he seen his wife so pleased; she turned as caring and dedicated as to be disgusting.

"Sorry you needed my money to make you love me, baby, I don't like it that way, I really don't."

"Why so fussy? We all know that riches make life easier. Besides, who said I don't care for you? I absolutely love you, darling," and she kissed him passionately as though to assure him of her feelings.

"No," Norman pushed her away. "It won't work for me," and went out just in time to miss one of her lovers' call.

Whatever, he didn't love his wife anymore and that's probably why he fell for Raven, a pretty starlet who had a role in one of the films based on his novels. She played a young runaway who gets in trouble and ends up with her body horribly mutilated.

The girl was cheerful, sweet, dressed like a hippie, did lots jogging and had long hair held up by a silver hairpin.

"It belonged to my granny," she said once and invited him to take it off.

Beautiful ebony curls fell upon her shoulders and he couldn't avoid stroking them. Then his fingers touched her lips… he was dying to kiss her.

"I can't forgive you for what you've done to me," she giggled one evening while they had a drink together.

"If I had known you before, I'd have changed the end," he smiled, his eyes fixed on hers.

"I guess that's enough to pardon you and invite you to my place."

The night was theirs and also the ones that followed until the shooting of the film was over.

It had been a long time since he felt so relaxed and had more fun than pressure while working. He wondered if Raven considered the fluctuant affair serious. Probably not, for she was very young and never talked about settling down.

Her image kept flashing before him during his journey home and also afterwards; the girl had bewitched him.

Norman did his best to resist her and it took him a while to get back to his usual life. His editors gave him a hand as his late success made them greedy of his talent and they commissioned other books; he had to work incessantly while Alyssa was relishing the huge amount of money available.

Neither ever talked about divorce; for sure, she would never give him up.

He recalled when a few months before the tragedy, while going through the pages of the book that made him so famous, a scribbled note caught his attention. 'Come back to me, I love you.'

It was Raven's handwriting. Why didn't she tell him before? Had she given him the time to find out about his true feelings and be free from any ties?

Many were the questions, doubts and, most of all, regrets. He should have divorced long ago. Everything around him appeared unfamiliar, distant; Alyssa seemed even more superficial and insensitive and shamefully naughty. A sudden, intense hate for her seized him and, for the first time, he wished she were dead.

The thought was horrid, terrifying, but he couldn't help it.

Had he really killed his wife after all?

If free, he would have searched for Raven, perhaps, in some youth hostel, flea market or on a solitary beach; she was waiting for him and he had to find her.

"Well, darling, doesn't this rain remind you anything?" Alyssa's ghost asked showing up once again.

"Go away; you're out of my life now."

"Thanks to you, love," she sneered and vanished.

Norman leaned forward to put his head in his hands. How could he go on like that?

After her apparitions, memories crammed his mind and a severe headache always followed. Everything happened so suddenly, accidentally, that damned night... He should have never consented to her request.

"We'll have the time to talk things over, to ponder if it's worth going on together, darling..." his wife said while packing.

Her words surprised him. For the first time she said something sensible... Norman didn't trust her, though.

Once at the cottage, she showed him a revolver.

"Just brought it along in case some weirdo shows up, with all that we hear in the news, we've got to be cautious."

The place was isolated, but he didn't like the idea of Alyssa having a gun. Could she wish him dead too? She spent lots of nights out these days; surely with one of her toy boys who made her have fun and sex at her own expenses. Had they conjectured something together?

The evening was spent dining on the terrace and sipping martinis and champagne. Now and then there was a tight smile, an inquisitive glance deep into one another's soul as if ever they had a soul... The alcohol wasn't enough to soothe their restlessness.

The weather didn't help much as dark clouds were billowing above and the lake's delicate breeze was turning into chilly gusts.

From the moment Norman found the note, he hadn't get Raven out of his mind. He even made her the protagonist of his latest novel just to feel her closer. He would have done anything to have her.

They were about to retire when Alyssa smiled alluringly and moved next to him, "It would be fun spending the night on the lake and so romantic…"

The tone was exaggeratedly mellifluous.

So she did have a plan… Once out there, she would kill him and gain possession of his money, free to squander it as she liked.

"The weather isn't good and I'm quite tired," he replied, visibly tense.

"Come on now, what can be more exciting than sailing through a storm?"

She got hold of a bottle of champagne, headed towards the dock and jumped on the boat, followed by her husband, eager to find out what she really had in mind.

The ripples weren't exactly waves yet and a few stars shone above; the weather looked as moody as his wife and he wished he were miles away, in Raven's arms…

Once on board, Alyssa began drinking heavily and when they were far from the shore, she muttered, "I know you've fallen out of love with me, but I still care for you, sweetie, couldn't imagine my life without you."

Her words upset him. She was lying.

"Do you say that to your lovers too?"

"How foolish, I simply have some fun once in a while."

Outrageous! Was she diverting herself by provoking him before firing? He definitely detested her.

It began raining heavily, strong gusts shook the vessel and the waves unbalanced it. Alyssa, already

12

unsteady through many drinks, was thrust into the water. Immediately, she started shouting and gasping. Norman seemed paralysed; he kept staring at the lifebuoy while his wife was imploring him to launch it...

'Hurry, Norman, what's keeping you? She's drowning,' a voice inside cried, but he didn't move... A sly smile only showed on his face. His wish was coming true...

The night grew very dark, the stars had vanished and Alyssa had disappeared into the murky depths.

When he recovered, he was lucid enough to throw the buoy into the water... just to avoid unpleasant suspicions.

Despite the researches, the body was never found and Norman was not charged with murder, but never would he have imagined that his only witness would become his ghastly prosecutor.

The first apparition occurred a few nights afterwards; Alyssa's body was swollen, like a grotesque carnival inflatable; the lips, blue and enormous, revolting.

"Why did you do this to me?" the spectre cried, "I'll find out and get even with you."

Norman leapt up, terrified, but there was only a pool of rancid smelling liquid was on the floor.

The uncanny visits became a true haunt. At first he considered them hallucinations and also saw a doctor, but it didn't help. Alyssa would never leave him in peace.

He was so devastated and depressed that he stopped writing and was on the point of taking his life when Raven knocked on his door. The news of Alyssa's death had reached her.

No questions were asked or secrets revealed. They moved in together, deeply in love; the girl overwhelmed with joy; it was too late to die now.

"I know why you did it," Alyssa said one night. "That bitch had already devoured your heart and you would have done anything for her... even let me die. You won't get away with it, Norman, you won't," and returned to her watery grave before he could object.

True, Raven had raptured him, but he didn't plan his wife's demise... it just happened... Even if he had launched that bloody buoy, she might have died all the same.

The spectre's last words, however, returned to him like a sinister premonition that overshadowed his happiness.

A few days later, Raven's body was found mutilated in the tub, just as described in Norman's story.

This time investigations were more accurate and the guy without any evidence to prove his innocence was locked in jail where Alyssa visited him for the last time.

"Satisfied now?" he sneered.

"Not enough, hon, still have to get even with you," and immediately she tightened her clammy hands around his neck.

"Want to watch you gasp and turn blue just like I did," she cried and kept laughing coarsely until his last breath.

The prisoner's macabre end remained inexplicable, but didn't cause much surprise. Jailors were used to strange murders within the prison walls.

The Symonds Yat Jumper

Geoff Nelder

Cecil used to hike up this meandering limestone trail on family picnic days twenty years ago. They were in the summer too, although not early evening like today. He liked to come here because of the silly name. Apparently, Symonds was a Sheriff of Hereford many centuries ago. In his boyhood Cecil wondered if Symonds wore a tin badge like the only other sheriffs he'd seen on TV. Just around that grey boulder and he'd see the gorse with its bright yellow blooms. Yes, he could see the rocky top, another twenty metres. The last walk of his life.

He loved it. More fresh air than he could breathe and it was free. No one to charge and add interest. He looked down the steep limestone cliff at the horseshoe bend of the River Wye, a hundred and twenty-five metres below. Cecil stretched his thin, tall body upwards, dressed in his best estate-agent black suit, forbidding his vertigo to grab a hold. His blond hair waved in the breeze, saying goodbye to over a hundred thousand pounds of student debt. He'd told his eager parents that there was no point him doing a five-year medical course when all he wanted to do was sell houses. Not that he made enough at the estate agency to pay off his gambling let alone student loan debts. It would have helped if Debbie had returned the eight-grand diamond engagement ring when she dumped him the previous week. He could've paid off Tony's heavies. They'd not find him here up Symonds Yat rock. Nor will anyone else in a few minutes. Just his broken body down there. Not in the River Wye either, unless he took a huge running jump so as to leap outwards and flap his arms like a maddened pterodactyl.

What's this, a delicate red flower in a limestone crack. A bloody cranesbill, really a wild kind of geranium. His favourite bloom to see him off. He stepped gingerly to the edge and became a touch dizzy. This was it. No doubts. There was a rock ten metres down that he might hit as he plummeted. Could be painful and messier than he'd imagined. A small run up then, there was so little room up on this pinnacle anyway. He took a few steps back, bent to a running poise and tensed his muscles. He gave himself a short countdown starting at three. No, five.

Five.

Four… good that there wasn't much wind on this balmy August day.

Three… nor rain. He was going to enjoy flying through the air.

Two… should he close his eyes on the way down, especially in the last second. God, it only took just over five seconds to hit the ground from this height, an app told him.

One… what was that?

A girl's voice, "Oi, get on with it, you prick!"

Eyes wide open now, he looked back down the winding path. Five metres away a young woman with spiky, bottle-red hair and ripped black clothes.

17

Been in a fight, or fashion? Damn, she was crowding him and she was standing on the cranesbill!

He called back to her, "It's too late to save me."

"Not trying to. Jump, you ponce. You're in the way."

He shook his head as if that assisted clarity. "In the way? You need access to the summit. Fieldwork?"

If she didn't scowl, she'd have a pretty face, even with that white makeup and black lips. "You havin' a laugh? I wanna jump too!"

Cecil staggered, which took him a little closer to the edge. "You too? Two suicides in one day from this beauty spot. It's a bit of a coincidence, isn't it?"

"Nah, there's bones down there. Some think they're just sheep but I knows better. Our school calls this 'Symonds Jump' Anyway, hurry up in case my drugs wear off."

Good lord, she was off her head. Maybe just a bit of speed for courage, or bennies to help with the climb. He'd be the gentleman. "You can go first, or we could jump together."

"I wanna see 'ow you do it. So if you muck it up…" Her black lips made a slanted gash.

"Right. I was thinking it might be a plan to run at it, to properly leap outwards." He looked back at the edge and down. "There's a nasty rock just there. Do you want to see?"

"Yeah, right, so while I'm eyeballing it you give us a helpful shove. I'll take your dodgy word for it. We've got to take a running jump."

18

Great bells, the girl was actually making a joke. He turned to face her and nearly smiled. "I'm Cecil, by the way. Estate agent. Huge debts. You?"

"Hi, Cecil By-the-way. Allegro, student dropout. Nothing to live for."

He looked down at his feet. Found another red cranesbill, crushed this time by his own shoes. Damn. "Allegro is a musical term for lively, isn't it?"

"I don't feel full of life, clever clogs. I want it over, get me? Now jump."

"Look at you, Allegro. You're a young, attractive... well, you could be under that muck. A whole life—"

"Hitting on me, you perve? A Cecil, at your age too. You're worse than my landlord and I came up here to delete everything."

"I know what you're doing. Samaritans, are you? Using reverse psychology on me. It won't work. Hey, who's that?"

She looked around, down the rough, winding path. "I didn't hear nothing."

Perhaps he was mistaken. The air whispering its disapproval of his intentions. Breezy, as it always was on hilltops.

"It's a man," Allegro said and took a few steps towards Cecil, for safety, perhaps. Irony.

A deep voice made its way up the fifty metres to them. "You two natterers. If you're going to do a lovers' leap, get on with it. It'll be dark soon."

Cecil glanced at his fake Rolex. It won't be sunset for another four hours. He'd meant to experience another kind of dark. The man had

19

rounded the corner. Shorter than himself, grey, but full and wavy hair. Blue jacket with red around the shoulders. Bus driver by the looks. Stagecoach Buses.

Cecil called down to him. "Don't tell me you're here to throw yourself off. If so, join the queue. Make a change for you to do that, won't it?"

Allegro sniggered, "I've seen you driving the 33 from Hereford. You chucked me off last week for no reason!"

He squinted at her. "Yeah, you pinched an old lady's handbag and swore like a trooper when you was caught red-handed. I got into trouble over you. More trouble…"

She muttered her response but Cecil only heard the words 'innocent', 'fucking', 'business'. He imaged the bus scene and caught reasons why these two were up Symonds Yat.

"I'm Cecil, she's Allegro, and you, sir?"

"Never you mind. How long?" He took a few steps closer.

The girl put a finger on her chin to aid her memory. "The old bag on the bus called him Eric. Eric Jones."

Cecil nearly held out his hand but stopped himself in the quandary over protocol when intending suicides meet. "Well, we're all here, Mr Jones, but surely you could go back down and continue driving people around? You do a good public service. Or is there something else wrong? Are you ill?"

"Nosey bugger, aren't you? I messed up, if you want to know." He pointed at Allegro. "After that fracas, I was upset. Took to drinking too much, didn't I? I crashed into a damn bus-stop this morning. Saw passengers on the floor so I legged it. I… I…"

Cecil took a step towards him. "They might have just been knocked down. It's bad but you had cause and can get help. Even if in…" Could he say 'prison'?

Allegro walked to Eric and put an arm around his shoulders. "Soz, driver. But hey, if you killed anyone it'd be on the news. Nothing on my feeds. Hey, Cesspit, how about we go to the Log Cabin café at the carpark? I'm dying for a coke."

What? The contrary notion upset the order in Cecil's mind for today. He dithered, then still properly undecided, agreed.

Eric led the way down with Allegro following Cecil, perhaps to make sure he didn't U-turn and ran up and over the top. He had looked back, wistfully as if he thought that fate urged him up and now a different random chance was taking him down.

***

They found a corner in the more-dead-than-alive café smelling of cheap coffee. At least the place was well-lit and a good attempt had been made to recreate the American roadside eatery look with chrome and red-faux-leather only cracked a little. Eric and Cecil risked builders' tea while Allegro took a Pepsi and ordered fries for all of them. "Counter-suicide food," she announced.

"Are you sure?" Cecil said, not finding any fat and salt data on the menu.

"Better," Eric grumbled, "than a mouthful of grit and broken teeth."

They all nodded their agreement. The conversation died while Allegro slurped and the men blew on their tea.

A streetlamp flickering on outside the window spurred Cecil to look at his watch. Seven-thirty already. If these two had a Samaritans agenda to thwart his suicide, they'd achieved it... for today. He didn't like the dark and he knew from a bad childhood memory that Symonds Yat had no lights. Black as sin at night. Treacherous path. He smiled at his own irony but the truth was that he wanted to jump clean off the top, not stumble and break a leg in a ditch.

Allegro burst into his thoughts with a slow, dangerous comment, "Cess... I could get that ring back for you. No probs. In fact, Eric would help me, wouldn't you?"

Eric choked on a chip. "I would?" She must have kicked him under the table. "Course. Eh?"

Cecil looked at them both. "Do you two know each other?"

Allegro jumped in. "No, well only vaguely. Like I said before. He owes me and I like you, Cess. Plus... I have skills."

Cecil was sure she had.

Allegro played with the chunky rings on her fingers. "Debbie, her name was. Right? Debbie...?"

"Arnold, but just a minute. I'd not told you two about that engagement ring, had I?"

22

"Yeah, you did. Didn't he, Eric? You can take me to the back of her house can't you?"

Eric was clearly disturbed at this volunteering to break and enter. "Well... I suppose... tomorrow?"

After telling her the address, although for the life of him he couldn't figure how he'd blurted it all out, they agreed to meet up at the café the next day at the same time.

By the time he'd reached his dismal flat, he was so tired he went straight to bed and slept better than he'd had for years.

Next morning he was chirpy and energised, especially after coffee and an unhealthy fry-up breakfast he normally couldn't be bothered to do. He should forget Debbie and download that app for hopeful middle-agers, what was it, Tinkle? No. eHarmony, that was it. Damn. It wanted him to register. So many bloody people want to know too much about you before you even browse. He'd google for another one. While he was making a pig's ear of tapping with fingers too thick for the phone's keys, he thought of those two the previous day.

How kind. And clever. Hey, he could look up that bus accident of Eric's and see if there really was good news for him.

Nothing for yesterday or earlier in the week. He frowned. Surely Eric wouldn't have made it up. He was devastated. And his uniform looked genuine enough for a Stagecoach bus driver. He tried typing in Eric Jones bus-driver, then sat back in shock. He threw his phone on the table, knocking over his coffee. He stood to fetch a cloth but stopped and picked up the phone again. News from four years ago: Eric Jones (55), died after leaping off Symonds Yat Rock before his trial for dangerous driving, driving under the influence and manslaughter. Two passengers waiting at a bus stop…

Cecil sat heavily back down in his chair. His head was buzzing, near to blacking out. He couldn't process it. Eric was alive yesterday. And he was out today helping Allegro. Just a minute. He cleared Google and thought. He didn't know her surname but there couldn't be many with that first name.

A minute later he stood and stared at his phone. Sweat broke out on his forehead. She had been twenty-two when she stabbed a shop assistant. Never caught. Her body was found near the base of Symonds Yat Rock six years ago. And he'd sent her around to his ex's house to break in and…

He ran out of the house then stopped. It was at least half an hour's run. He should call Debbie. He tried but he'd been blocked. The police. He cancelled just as it started to ring. What was he going to say? 'Excuse me but two dead people with histories of violence have been sent around to the house of my ex-fiancée by me. You can find me at Symonds Yat walking around near the café, in circles, shouting to myself.'

He didn't call the police. Nor anyone. He turned up at the café just after five. He didn't expect the other two to appear but he bought two teas and a cola anyway. Crisps instead of fries, so it didn't matter being cold.

The café bell tinkled and he looked up. There they were, as if alive. Eric with his blue and red driver's uniform. Allegro, smiling, with her torn black cape over a mauve miniskirt and green tights.

They sat and sipped. Crunched.

"I know who you both are, or were."

Allegro still smiled. "We thought you might look us up. We can't cross, you see. We have to save someone from jumping there in order for our souls to find peace."

"Really? What if you fail and I jump anyway? Today or next year?"

She popped another ready-salted into her mouth and spoke, showering the table with bits. "Then we'd be back in limbo, probably with you. So, do us a favour, will you, dear Cesspot? Stay alive. Find another Debbie. Hey, you should've seen her yesterday, eh, bus driver?"

Eric put his tea down and grinned. A tooth was missing. "Yeah, she went white and screamed. Like she'd seen a ghost."

Cecil's stomach knotted. How terrible. He stood and so did they.

Allegro started to say something about looking up old friends but stopped when her hands and feet faded. So did Eric's limbs. Both slowly vanished before his eyes. As did his surprisingly calm demeanour. Now his mind whirled along with his stomach.

Perhaps that meant they'd now passed over. Whatever that meant. A clinking noise on the table made him glance down. The emerald ring rocked then stopped. At least he could hock it and pay off his debts. Start again.

His hand went to pick it up. Strange. He couldn't grasp it. Of course he couldn't... not with hands that were fading away.

Dead Men Do Tell Tales

Jason R Frei

The fog rolled in thick, like midnight slumber, covering everything in its wake. Even the lights at the end of the dock sputtered and choked. The stench of the sea pervaded the city. At this hour, people either slept or drank.

An old seaman with a grizzled beard stumbled out of *The Fisherman's Catch*. He took a few steps forward and then lilted to the left, where he landed square up against a light post, hard enough to send the flame dancing like a witch around a bonfire. The seaman blinked his eyes several times and then fished in his coat for a stained nicotine pouch. He rolled himself a cigarette, spilling most of the tobacco. He inhaled deeply and smoked the cigarette down to his fingertips in one breath. He let the smoke out in a slow, controlled spurt where it swirled and eddied with the thickening fog.

The old man coughed and spat a thick wad of phlegm onto the splintered wooden sidewalk. He steadied himself upright, hitched up his pants and walked down to the shoreline. His head spun and he couldn't remember which way was home.

He walked through the sand to the water's edge where he knelt down and cupped water over his face to clean the inebriation from his head. He saw a dark shadow in the fog ahead of him. Thrusting his head forward, he squinted to make out a shape.

Realization struck like a gong and he quickly shuffle-rolled across the sand like a crab with broken legs. From out of the fog came a schooner, running full tilt into the sand where the old seaman had been. He sobered up instantly and ran back to the inn.

The schooner was in horrible condition. It was a wonder it had made it to the beach at all. The name on the bow was almost illegible, but one veteran dockhand recognized the ship as *The Seaport,* a fishing vessel very popular in the area. Its splintered aft mast lay broken in two on the deck. The fore sail flapped in tatters. Most of the hull was blackened by intense fire. It looked like the ship may crumble at any moment.

Several men boarded the boat to look for the crew. Bodies lay strewn across the deck. They found a crewman lashed to the ship's wheel, still alive. The men untied him, but he stuck fast. Long iron nails pierced his hands, holding him to the wheel. When one man tried to remove a nail, the crewman shrieked wildly. His shrieks turned to whimpers and then to sobbing. The men aboard heard him mumbling. One brave soul crept closer to listen.

"Bramble, it was," said the crewman. "The devil himself--Cap'n Elias Bramble. His soul, darker than coal."

The rest of the men slowly made their way forward. One offered the spiked crewman a flask. He tilted his head back, thankful for the drink. The skin on half of his face was flayed off, exposing raw nerves, swollen muscle and bone. One eye socket stared emptily and his remaining eye was a milky white. The crewman gulped down the spirits and continued.

"A fog just like this one had come in fast. Our fine Cap'n Decker was already sick—so hoarse he couldn't even whisper. He was in his Quarter's, resting. We had just thrown the nets when Bramble drove *The Maybell* right into our port side. The dogs were on us before we knew it."

The sailor's face writhed in agony for a moment, reliving the memory. His tongue sucked at the back of his throat and horrible, wet grunts issued from his broken mouth. The flask was offered again.

"That was good, sir," the crewman said. "Just like Cap'n Decker's special we used to drink after a big haul. But there weren't no rum that day. Bramble and his men were vicious. We're just fishermen, not soldiers. We were slaughtered. Cap'n Decker came out and ran straight at Bramble. Halfway across the deck, *The Seaport* lurched. The Cap'n got caught up in the rigging and went right overboard. Everyone else was dead or dying. Bramble's men tacked me to the wheel. They took everything we owned, set the ship alight and sailed off. And by God, sir, as soon as that devil left, the fog went with him.

The fisherman sat very still. Only the wheezing in his chest gave away the fact that he was still alive. He then threw his head back abruptly and let loose an awful, gurgling howl. Water spewed forth from his broken maw. He tore one hand from the wheel and forcibly wrenched his head to the side, breaking his own neck with a horrendous crunch. His tongue lolled out of his mouth and his body drooped forward. It was at that same moment that a man at the stern of the ship screamed.

Everyone surged toward the sound. The screaming man held a rope that he hauled up from the side. The lifeless body of Captain William Decker was attached to the end of the rope by his feet. A rictus of torment spread across his contorted face. Water issued from his ghastly, twisted lips. Once the last drop fell to the deck, a ghostly voice emanated from the ship and uttered the words "I'm coming for you."

***

Captain Bramble and his depraved cutthroats were caught up in a night of drunken revelry at *The Half Moon*. The drink flowed like an untamed river. Women danced and cavorted like wild beasts in heat. The sounds of bawdy and raucous laughter carried all the way down at the docks. Outside, the wind started up like a howling banshee. It rippled down the streets, blowing trash and debris aside like parting a crowd.

Bramble sat in the corner. His thick, black moustache curled up at the ends, like a devilish smile. He wore his finest clothing, made of colourful dyed silk, damask and velvet. Upon his head sat a large, cocked hat made of beaver fur. Ostrich feathers strut up from the side. The front peak was cleft and wrapped with golden thread, giving the hat the appearance of having horns.

Rings adorned each finger. Two thick golden chains piled around his neck and a gold hoop dangled from his left ear. His leather breaches were tucked into his supple, black boots. His coat was long and black with intricate gold stitched threads.

He sat between two drunken, nubile women who laughed at every word he said. He told stories of his recent forays, including each of his men by name to keep them interested. His tales were graphic and violent, but he carried on the conversation as if he were an orator reciting epic poetry. His animated hands made the adventures come to life. Men and women lingered over his every word and sat closer and closer to be involved in his storytelling.

Just as Bramble was getting to the best bit, the door banged open and startled everyone in the tavern. The silence lasted only for a moment before everyone broke out in laughter, louder than it needed to be. Only Captain Bramble remained silent. He cocked his head to the side, like he was listening to a whispering in his ear.

"Close that damn door," shouted the barman over the sounds of laughter and wind.

"Henry," said Bramble to his Quartermaster. "Go check *The Maybell* and make sure her moorings are fast. I don't want this damned wind taking my ship."

Henry did as he was told and took three others with him. They swayed from side to side as they bawled their drunken songs.

Bramble smiled less and less as the festivities continued. After some time, most of his men passed out at their tables or on the floor. Some went upstairs with the women. Bramble sat alone. He sat and watched the door.

The night deepened. A thick blanket of fog wound its way through the streets, forcing itself into every crack and crevice until the whole town was lost in its haze. It was a heavy and tenebrous thing. It clung to the body like a funeral shroud. Bramble saw it pushing up against the windows of the tavern and he imagined it peering inside at him. Strange shapes danced through its murk. He heard whispers, like little melodies tugging at his ear.

Bramble shook ever so slightly from time to time, as if a chill slowly crawled up and down his spine. His eyes roamed around the room. They settled for a few moments on the door before starting their travels again. He heard the fog against the window, pressing and slithering across the glass. Bramble shrank further into his chair, forcing himself against the wall.

A tendril of smoky fog snaked its way under the door, exploring the joints, cracks and knots in the wooden floor. When it seemed satisfied, the vapors rose and coalesced. They formed a vague outline of a man. The details grew sharper and the form raised an arm and pointed at Bramble, who shook hard enough to rattle the table. The form raised its leg to take a step and the tavern door flew open, disrupting the smoke and causing it to dissipate.

Bramble jumped to his feet and drew his pistol as Henry rushed through the door, panicked and afraid. Henry stopped dead in his tracks. Bramble's eyes had a far-away look in them, as if he were on the brink of insanity.

"Captain," yelled Henry. "Are you alright?"

Bramble shook the confusion from his head. His eyes focused on Henry and he slid his pistol back into his sash.

"What is it, Henry?" Bramble's voice wavered.

"We checked on *The Maybell*, sir. Her moorings stood fast through the storm, but we couldn't see any crewmen on deck. We checked below and found them in their hammocks." Henry paused and licked his dry lips. "They're dead sir, all dead."

Bramble woke his men and they went together to *The Maybell*. Bramble walked slowly and his hands shook, but he led his crew as a show of courage. By now, the men heard what happened and they were scared. Bramble set foot first on the ship and was the first to go below deck.

Before the night's debauchery, Bramble ordered four sailors to stay with the frigate. All four lay cocooned in their hammocks, wool blankets pulled up to their chins. Their ashen white faces stared with bulging eyes and protruding tongues. Bramble went to the closest and pulled down the blanket. A length of rope wound around the man's neck.

Without warning, all four men sat up. Water cascaded from their mouths like miniature waterfalls. Their heads turned to the Captain, bones cracking in their necks. In unison, their mouths moved and a liquid, burbling voice issued from their collective throats.

"I'm coming for you."

***

Those among Bramble's men that had any semblance of religion crossed themselves and scrambled to get away. The heathens among them turned tail and ran as fast as possible. Bramble turned quickly and tripped over a loose cable, crashing to the floor. He skittered on all fours and clambered up the ladder.

He emerged on the deck as the fog drastically thickened. Its shadowy moisture enveloped him. A cacophony of sounds and lights banged and flashed all around him. It sounded like the ship was under attack. Shadowy figures crept through the fog, just out of sight. One of his own men ran past, screaming, blood dripping from his head. Thunder rumbled and large raindrops poured down from the sky. Bramble pulled his cutlass as a shape stepped forth from the gloom.

Captain William Decker stood before him, the ghastly smile still frozen on his face. Without issuing a challenge, the wraith thrust his spadroon at Bramble's midsection. The pirate barely got his cutlass up in time to deflect the blow. He noticed the out-of-place weapon and knew instantly that he was no ordinary fisherman. The spadroon was the weapon of a Patriot naval commander during the Revolution. He was fighting a war hero.

Decker saw the surprise in Bramble's eyes and pressed his attack. The privateer countered and attacked back. The fight seemed endless with neither one gaining an advantage over the other. The storm raged on. Back and forth, they clashed swords up and down the entire deck as lightning flashed and thunder rumbled.

Bramble ran up against the quarterdeck with nowhere to go. Decker raised his spadroon for a killing blow. There was a deafening report and the specter staggered backwards. Bramble's pistol jutted from his off hand, smoke still curling from its barrel. With a vicious howl, he leapt forward.

A peal of thunder shook the boat and lightning ripped from the sky, hitting the ship's main mast. Bramble toppled to the deck. He crawled to the taffrail to haul himself up. The ship heaved again and the captain collided into the capstan. The levers snapped and ropes tumbled down, snaring him. Lightning hit the deck, throwing a shower of splinters like shrapnel.

Decker approached, slow and easy, taking his time. The pirate captain got to his knees, praying and begging

"God, please forgive me. My soul can be saved."

Decker laughed.

"Not even God can save you," he said, throat raw and raspy from the sea water.

Decker grabbed the rope and tied it tight around Bramble's legs. He dragged his foe to the lee side and threw him over. The captain screamed as he fell, but stopped short of the water by mere inches. There he bobbed up and down. The waves crashed mercilessly, battering him against the side of the ship and filling his open mouth.

***

The storm lasted for six days. *The Maybell* heaved from side to side in her berth, but remained moored. Lightning set all three sails ablaze and they became a beacon of light in the darkness of the storm and fog.

On the sixth day, the storms subsided and the fog cleared. People ventured out of their homes to assess the damage. The barman from *The Half Moon* told the constable that Bramble and his men had gone out to *The Maybell*, but no one saw them return.

The constable and three watchmen boarded the ship. The sails were nothing more than ash and the masts were cinders. Charred holes shot through the deck. Timber and rope cluttered it. Not a soul could be found on board, either on deck or below.

Finally, the peacekeepers came to the Captain's quarters. The door was locked, but a few sharp blows from a wrench opened it up. Entering the Captain's quarters, a strong smell of mould and dirty seawater assaulted the men. Covering his mouth and nose with a handkerchief, the constable inspected the room.

A large solid wooden table littered with maps, coins, jewelry and cloth sat in the center of the room. Behind the table stood the Captain's chair with a full bottle of wine next to it. It was if the storm that raged outside had not touched this room.

A single set of salt-encrusted boot prints led to the bed chamber. The constable opened the bed chamber door. Lying in the bed was Elias Bramble, the pirate captain of *The Maybell*. A noose coiled around his neck. His eyes stared open wide if he had glimpsed Hell itself. Seated in a chair at the foot of the bed reposed the corpse of Captain William Decker. He held the end of the noose in his own gnarled hand. His mouth no longer twisted into a malformed grimace. Instead, he wore a tranquil smile, finally at rest.

Shivering the Timbers

David Turnbull

John Andrew Mercer, otherwise known as Johno, was two days short of his twentieth birthday when he drew his last breath. The first bullet passed straight through him, punching a hole in the wall and embedding itself in the wooden beam behind. The bullet took something with it. Yanked it violently from Johno's physical body. A small fragment which contained the essence of him. The raw material from which ghosts construct themselves.

He was conscious from the first instant. Saw, like some Peeping Tom, through the forced channel of bullet hole to where Malkie Hamilton stood over his body. Malkie was the enforcer for the *boys*. He was dressed in a black Crombie and brown brogues. Johno watched as he pressed the homemade silencer barrel of the gun against the skull of his fallen physical body and pulled the trigger once more for good measure.

Saw his smug executioner take out a Polaroid camera and take several snaps of the executed corpse. Saw the little tremble of satisfaction that ran through the man as he dropped the barely dried photos into his pocket. These would surely appear on leaflets shoved through letter boxes on the estate back home. A dire warning to anyone who might be tempted to step out of line.

When Johno thought of his mother and sisters seeing him there on that dirty floor, mouth open, blood from the entry wound pooling around his broken head, he was filled with such rage it sent a little hairline fissure snaking up the grain of the beam.

Later, after Malkie had departed, Johno watched two nervous teenagers hurriedly rolling his cold, stiff cadaver in a moth-eaten rug, wrapping the rug in plastic, carrying it away. Obediently following orders that came down through the chain of command to compliant soldier boys like them.

Later still he saw the woman in the blue overalls who came with a bucket of hot, soapy water and a scrubbing brush to scour away his bloodstains from the floor. He watched her drop the smoking butt end of the cigarette that had hung from her waxy red lip in to the wan, pink water that contained the last of his mortal existence.

Later yet came the tradesman, who used his pliers to yank out the bullet casing from the beam and his trowel to plaster over the bullet hole. The *boys* had fingers in many pies and many people to do their bidding.

Time passed.

Johno brooded in the beam.

For a long, long he was trapped in darkness behind the mended plaster, a tiny, tiny grain, a fragment of conscious dust embedded in what looked like a bevelled knot. But slowly, slowly he began to expand, spreading like wet rot vertically and horizontally. For a while he resembled a mildewed crucifix. Given the circumstances which

39

led to his murder the irony of that imagery was not lost on him.

That shape could not, however, hold him for long. He knew no bounds. He was uncontainable. He spread like butter, and seeped like sump oil, and crept relentlessly into the very fabric of the house. He was like a rabid fungus, seizing ever more territory. And when he was out of the beams and joists and at last into the floorboards and the skirting, and the frames he saw everything. All the comings and goings, the plots and the machinations, the torture and mutilations that went on in that dreadful house.

Johno was omnipresent. Like a God in his own architecturally contained universe.

And, like a vengeful God, he patiently planned his revenge.

***

Malkie Hamilton was a big lumbering bastard of a skinhead. Ben Sherman shirt, yellow braces, drainpipe Levi's, oxblood Doc Martens, tattoo of William of Orange on his bullish neck. Face pitted in acne, built like a delinquent rugby player, barrel chest and ham hock thighs. The raw, meaty bulk of him filled the narrow stone gunnel with aggressive belligerence. Johno felt paralyzed as the shadow of his tormentor fell over him. A cold, Belfast wind howled around the two of them like a Banshee come down from the hills.

"The *boys* say you've got till tomorrow morning to get out of town," he told Johno.

40

"Have a heart," said Johno. "Sure, I'm only sixteen, so I am. Where I am I to go? What about my Ma? What about my wee sisters?"

Malkie cracked the hairy knuckles on his pork sausage fingers. He leaned in and pressed his nose menacingly against Johno's. His breath reeked of Woodbine cigarettes. "Ye should have thought about that before ye started fraternizing with Catholics."

"Sure, I'm not fraternizing, Malkie," said Johno. "It's about the music. I'm learning to play guitar, that's all. Can you not tell the *boys* that it's about the music?"

"Ye're strumming on your strings while they bomb our pubs," said Malkie, head-butting Johno without warning. Johno staggered backwards to the stone wall, blood gushing from the wound that had opened above his left eyebrow. "We're going to form a band," he persisted, wiping blood from his eyes with the sleeve of his denim jacket. "We'll be as big as the Boomtown Rats."

"The only band you should the thinking about is the one from the Orange Lodge that plays *The Sash My Father Wore,*" said Malkie, his harsh, guttural tones echoing along the close.

Johno spat out some blood that had trickled down into his mouth.

"Could you not just give me a wee warning?" he said. "Break a leg or something?"

"You're not welcome on the estate," said Malkie. "Who knows what you've been blabbing about to your papist pals with their safety pins and spikey fucking hair."

"I haven't been blabbing about anything," insisted Johno. "I don't know anything to blab about, for Christ sakes."

Malkie punched him hard in the gut. His feet went from under him. He slid down the wall and fell to the rain soaked ground. Malkie loomed over him, taking considerable pleasure in what he was doing. "Ye've got till tomorrow," he said and kicked Johno in the ribs. "Get on the ferry. Fuck off to London."

He turned to walk away, then paused as if he'd just had an afterthought.

"See how ye get on strumming a guitar now," he laughed, bringing his heel down hard on Johno's hand.

Johno lay there for a long time, clutching his injured hand to his belly, puddle water seeping into his jeans, blood rippling over his chin and staining his Buzzcocks' tee-shirt. Beyond the gunnel he could hear the slap of a rope against concrete and group of girls, braving the weather to chant a skipping song. He hoped his little sisters wouldn't see him. He hoped one day they'd forgive him for running out on them.

***

By day Johno worked as a labourer on a big construction project that was redeveloping parts of the Isle of Dogs in East London. By night he collected glasses at a music venue in Camden. He rented a bedsit in Chalk Farm. He tried to learn guitar from a tattered Bert Weedon tutorial he picked up in second hand book shop. But his fingers had healed badly. They gave him a lot of pain. He lacked manual dexterity he'd once had. He amassed a big pile of notepads with scribbled, impassioned lyrics that were cursed never be set to music.

He always had this nagging feeling that the *boys* weren't done with him. He took the necessary precautions. The letters he sent to his mother and sisters bore no return address. He travelled by tube to post them, making sure they'd be stamped with different postcodes. He set up a standing arrangement with one of his cousins to call the number of a Belfast city centre phone box every fourth Wednesday so he could check up on his family and they could relay messages back to him.

It was all to no avail. When the time came, the *boys* knew exactly where to find him.

Walking home one night after a late shift he was bundled into the back of a Ford Transit and taken to the house. Johno thought they'd crossed a bridge and maybe the house was in Streatham or Clapham. But he was never one hundred percent sure of its location.

Malkie Hamilton was waiting for him in that room, with its bare floors and bare walls and the black-out curtains which hid the sickening things that befell people like Johno who were brought there. In the four years since they'd last met Malkie had clearly prospered. He was still very much the hard man, but no longer a mere foot soldier. His Crombie and brogues looked expensive. His hair had grown out, no longer shaven to the scalp. He had gold rings on his fingers, a gold chain around his thick neck, a gold band around one hairy wrist, a gold watch the other.

"I'd offer ye a seat," he said when Johno was pushed into the room. "But as ye can see I've no seats to offer. Besides our business won't take that long."

"I've got no business with you," said Johno.

He heard the door shut and a key turn in the lock.

Malkie cracked his knuckles. "Oh, but you have. The *boys* are concerned about an informant. A couple of good lads are serving time on account of him."

Johno laughed nervously. "What's that got to do with me?"

"An example must be set," said Malkie.

He grinned, revealing a gold cap on one of his front teeth.

"Like I said," repeated Johno. "What's that got to do with me?"

Malkie casually produced his gun from inside his Crombie. Johno could tell from the way he held it that he'd had lots of practice. His fat index finger stroked the trigger with an unsettling tenderness. Johno could see scratches and scorch marks on the home made silencer that sheathed the barrel.

"How can the *boys* think I'm an informant?" said Johno. "Sure, I've been away for nearly four years. I don't know anything or anyone to inform on, so I don't."

Malkie shook his head. "It doesn't really matter. They need to make an example of someone. Who better than a known fraternizer?"

Johno clenched his fists to stop his hands from trembling. "This is ridiculous," he said. "The *boys* want me dead just to prove a point? They don't care if I'm innocent or not?"

Malkie shrugged his big shoulders. "Don't you go worrying about your Ma and your sisters," he said, testing the weight of the gun. "We know ye've been sending Postal Orders. But the *boys* won't leave them short. They'll be looked after once the deed is done. In fact, one or two of the *boys* have already been looking after your Ma, if you get my drift. And your sisters are ripening up just fine. Especially Deidre. Personally, I've had my eye on that one for some time now."

"You bastard!" yelled Johno and ran at him, feeble fists wildly flailing.

Malkie pushed him off easily. He raised the gun and pulled the trigger as nonchalantly as he might have done if he was ringing the bell on a bus to indicate he wanted to get off at the next stop.

***

Oh, the things Johno witnessed in that house of horror.

The pulling of teeth. The breaking of fingers. The shattering of kneecaps. The walls rang with screams. The timbers were drenched in blood. He saw guns wrapped in linen and hidden inside chimneys. He witnessed the construction of a crude incendiary device. He watched the men who planted it laugh and guzzle Guinness as the devastation wrought by their bomb played out on the news report being shown on a black and white TV.

Johno learned how to shiver the timbers. Sending out little ripples of vibration that shook the house and unsettled the bad men who lurked there like sleek rats in their lair. There was little satisfaction in it. Malkie Hamilton did not return and Johno's thirst for vengeance remained unquenched and unrequited.

As time passed the *boys* gave up the pretence of political idealism. It had always been a smokescreen for what was rotten at their core. Their cause was always their own self-interest. They brazenly became what they'd been all along. Criminals and gangsters.

For a while they were in league with a gang of West Indian Yardies. The house reverberated to reggae beats and reeked from top to bottom of Ganga. Forged banknotes filled the spaces behind the plaster on the walls. For another period of time they threw their lot in with people smugglers operating out of China Town. The house became a brothel. Fat bellied men would pay for sex with girls half their age who could barely speak a word of English.

Seeing in graphic detail what went on in those sordid rooms made Johno feel somewhat of a voyeur. He had still been a virgin when his life had been so unjustly stolen from him. There had been girls he'd taken back to his bedsit. There had been mutual groping and heavy petting. But none of them had gone all the way. None of them had stayed the night.

Another thing stolen from away him.

Another reason for him to hate Malkie Hamilton.

In frustration he would shiver the timbers and tremble the house from the foundations to the eaves. The flabby, naked men would grab their clothes and flee. The girls would curl up and shiver, muttering incantations in Cantonese to protect themselves from the angry spirit they believed inhabited the place in which they were incarcerated.

For a while there was an era of relative calm in the house. The *boys*, it seemed, were lying low. The house was converted into bedsits of the type Johno himself used to rent in Chalk Farm. A scruffy woman with barely concealed drink and drug addictions was installed in the basement flat as a sort of caretaker.

Tenants came and tenants went, filling their tiny, cramped rooms with meagre items unpacked from cardboard boxes and plastic bags, leaving without notice, disappearing in the dead of night to avoid settling their last week's rent. Johno watched events unfold with a lethargic dispassion. There was only one person he wished to see arriving. And that person it seemed might never return to the scene of his crime.

One day, however, a new tenant arrived and was allocated the room in which Johno had been murdered. A teenager of mixed race parentage. Carmel complexion, dark brown frizzy hair, leather jacket, huge belt, with an eagle shaped buckle, running though the loops of his stonewashed jeans.

He didn't have much by way of belongings. But his pride of possession was an acoustic guitar inside a guitar case covered in stickers with the names of bands Johno had never even heard of. The varnish on the guitar was scratched and worn. The frets had clearly seen many fingers.

The boy could play. Not just strum a few chords. He could play really well. Johno was in awe. He'd fill the windowsill and the skirting boards with his presence and watch for hours as the boy contorted his fingers to complex chord sequences and joyously strummed the strings with his plectrum.

Johno wished he could somehow find his old notepads and let the boy see the lyrics he wrote all those years back. He may not have had the musical ability to master an instrument, but he was pretty sure he'd had a good way with words. The music this talented boy was composing would have been the perfect accompaniment.

Something else which could never be because of Malkie Hamilton.

Johno had to content himself with listening and watching.

But there was a dirty little fly wriggling around in the ointment of the boy's life. It came in the form of the scruffy caretaker, with her fusty dresses and her baggy cardigans and her grey, anaemic skin. She was a corrupting influence. To raise money for her own habits she began supplying the boy with little coloured pills, tempting him ever deeper into her addled world of chemical dependency.

"Thank you," he'd say, handing over the extra payment on top of his rent in exchange for a week's supply. "I really need these to get my creative juices flowing."

"No, you don't!" Johno wanted to yell. *"You have a raw talent. It should be nurtured. Not squandered!"*

But he was impotent. Mute within the timbers.

Had Johno not been handicapped by such limitations he might have been able to avert the tragedy of the overdose. The boy became distracted and frustrated by a complex piece of music he was pushing himself to devise. He went several nights without sleeping. Lost track of how many pills he'd popped. Began behaving erratically. Vacillating between tear soaked sobbing and maniacal laugher.

When he set the guitar down and curled up on the bed Johno sensed this was a huge mistake. Knew with an unflinching certainty that if the boy fell into sleep he would never again wake up. He shivered the timbers and shook the room, trying desperately to rouse him. He knocked over the guitar, causing the sound box to bong loudly from the vibrations of the strings.

When this failed, he tried to rouse the other tenants, opening and slamming the door over and over, levering the floorboards so they toppled the wardrobe with a mighty crash. But the residents of the house were not the type to interfere with someone else's business. Most of them had business of their own they wouldn't want interfered with. They kept themselves to themselves in the hope that no one would pay any undue attention to them.

All that Johno achieved was the tenant of the next door bedsit thumping on the wall and yelling at the boy to *shut the fuck up*. Poor Johno was forced to watch as the boy gagged and puked and choked on his own vomit.

The injustice of this untimely death sent Johno into a rampage of rage, shattering joists and spitting splinters. Finally, down in her basement hovel, he found the woman. She was flaked out amongst the cheap cider stains on her mattress, greasy hair matted and stuck to the badly applied make up on her wan face.

Johno sprang the floorboards, popping out rusty nails and tumbling her rudely out of bed. Groggily she stumbled for the door, confused at what was happening. But Johno wasn't finished with her. He sent a crack shattering through the floor. It swallowed her left leg right up to her thigh, tearing the flesh and slicing an artery. The hot fountain of blood drenched the timbers. The house drank her blood with a vampiric gluttony.

Johno wished dearly that it might have been Malkie Hamilton.

* * *

The house fell silent.

There was a police investigation into the two deaths. Both were put down to misadventure through drug abuse. But the *boys* didn't like the attention. The house held too many of their dark secrets. They boarded up the place and left it to sit empty. All that Johno had for company were mice and spiders and the pigeons that roosted by the chimney breast.

He no longer looked in on the rooms. There was nothing left for him to see. It felt as if he had closed his eyes and drifted halfway to sleep. He mourned for the loss of the boy. His untimely death became a metaphor for all that was lost to Johno.

He had no idea of how many years had passed since he was shot. He wondered if by now he'd have been married. If he would have had children. If he would have been a good father. He wondered if his sisters had children. And if he would have been a good uncle. He wondered if his Ma was a good Grannie. He wondered if his Ma was still alive.

One day, however, the sound of the front door being opened and slammed back shut roused him from his fugue. He was drawn to the murmur of voices speaking in the hallway. And one in particular, a voice with an accent as broad and rough as a Saturday night boozer on a Belfast street.

The voice he had waited all these years to hear.

He observed from multiple angles and viewpoints. From the back of the door. From the banister of the stairwell. Looking up from the floorboards. Looking down from where a patch in the ceiling plaster had exposed the beams,

Three men stood there. Two, who looked to be in their early sixties, were dressed in suits and had the appearance of backstreet lawyers. Despite their advanced years and dapper attire, Johno recognized them immediately as the two teenagers who had been dispatched to dispose of his body.

The third man, the elder of the trio, was somehow more difficult for Jonno to be certain about. His head was almost bald. Wisps of a downy, grey combover swept across the shiny crown of his scalp. His face was drawn and haggard. He stood with shoulders hunched over a walking stick, held in an arthritic bird-like claw of a hand.

It wasn't till he spoke again that Jonno was finally certain it was him.

"I can't go to prison, lads," he said. "I've got diabetes and high blood pressure. I'm prone to kidney infections."

"You won't go to prison," said one of the suited men. "All you have to do is lie low here for few more days till we sort you out with a passport and fake ID."

"I'm not going somewhere hot, am I?" said the man Jonno now knew without a shadow of a doubt was Malkie Hamilton. "These days I don't do too well with the heat, so I don't."

"Don't worry about a thing," said the other suited man. "It's all in hand."

"Sure, I knew the *boys* would come through for me," said Malkie.

"All the *boys* who were around back in the day are six feet under," said the first suit, "but the new regime hasn't forgotten everything you did for the cause. You're a hero. They won't let you go down on evidence that's well past its sell by date."

"And they'll see that my daughter and my wee grandsons want for nothing once I'm away?" asked Malkie, his hand trembling slightly around the grip of the walking stick.

"Don't worry about anything, Gramps," repeated the second suit. "You just lie low here for a few days." He nodded to the large suitcase he'd dragged in behind him. "We've got you a portable DVD player and a stack of old westerns. There's beer and pork pies and sleeping bag. Tomorrow one of us will bring you some fish and chips."

Malkie shook his head. "Ah, sure, I knew the *boys* would look out for me."

Johno watched Malkie shuffling behind the men as they led him to one of the downstairs rooms. He clutched his walking stick for dear life. As if he would fall down if he let go of it. One of the men pulled off the plastic cover that had been draped over an armchair and eased him down into it. The other unpacked the suitcase, laying out cans of lager, a pack of supermarket pork pies and a large bag of crisps onto a dusty coffee table, before setting up the DVD player.

"All you have to do is open it like this," he said, giving a little demonstration. "Then you put in the DVD you want, shut the lid press play."

He brought out a pile of DVD's and set them on the table.

"They told us you like westerns," he said. "We got you a selection of John Wayne and Clint Eastwood."

"Sure, you're good lads, so you are," said Malkie, still holding his cane and looking incredibly frail within the armchair.

The other suited man had removed the plastic cover from the sofa. He unrolled a blue sleeping bag onto it. "When you're ready for a kip, lie down

53

here," he said. "The toilet is just across the hallway. We have keys. We'll let ourselves in when we come back tomorrow. No one else knows you're here. If anyone knocks on the door, don't answer it."

"Sure, I'll be as quiet as mouse, so I will," said Malkie, leaning forward to pull the ring on one of the cans.

***

Once the two suited men had left Malkie had two or three attempts at the DVD player before figuring out how to work it. He settled down to watch Rio Bravo, Dean Martin and Ricky Nelson co-starring with John Wayne.

His hands were awkward as they fumbled with the cellophane on the pack of pork pies. He ate noisily and messily, pie crust tumbling from his mouth to settle on the front of his grimy blue shirt. In the flickering glow of the movie, he looked like a shadow of his former self. He began crunching down on the crisps, stuffing his mouth full and washing them down with gulps of lager. He burped and farted. When he used a dirty thumb nail to wedge out a crisp fragment stuck in his nicotine stained teeth, Johno noticed the gap where the gold capped tooth had once sat.

He's pathetic, thought Johno.

No longer the skinhead thug who ran him out of town. No longer the seedily suave executioner who'd so callously taken his life. The dynamic between the two of them had intrinsically changed.

54

Now the balance of power was well and truly with Johno.

He could have ended it there and then. Sprung the floorboards and tipped the armchair so violently that Malkie Hamilton cracked open his ugly skull against the coffee table. Watched as he bled out and drew his last breath. But where was the joy in that? Where was the satisfaction? He wanted Malkie to tremble in fear. He wanted him to feel afraid. To experience the terror he himself had experienced.

He started small. The slow creaking of an un-oiled hinge on an upstairs door. Crick-crick-crick on the boards of the upstairs landing. Like someone walking, slowly creeping. He saw Malkie's fat hands stiffen and curve around the armrests of the armchair as he raised his head and looked in confusion and curiosity up at the ceiling.

Next Johno made each the stair thump in descending order. Then had them thump one after the other in ascending order. Malkie gripped his walking stick, groaned as he eased himself up from the armchair, went to the door and called into the darkness. "Did ye forget something, lads? Ye gave me a fright, so ye did."

Johno slammed one of the doors so loud it shook the walls.

"Who's there?" demanded Malkie. "I give ye due warning, ye've no idea who it is ye're messing with. I'm a notorious fucking gunman, so I am."

Johno juddered the coffee table and sent the pork pies and crisps flying. Malkie turned, rheumy eyes popping wide when he saw the lager that was glugging out from an overturned can. He used his

55

stick for balance, leaned over to place it upright. Johno slammed the door shut. Malkie yelped and jumped so hard it sent a spasm through his worn out back muscles.

"Just the wind," he muttered out loud when he saw the closed door. "There's a window left open somewhere. Ye're giving yourself the willies, silly auld bugger that ye are."

Now Johno split the wood in the door panel, spelling out his name in jagged crevasses and fissures. *John Andrew Mercer*. Adding in brackets *(JOHNO)*, in case his adversary wasn't one hundred percent sure of who he was dealing with.

Seeing this, Malkie gasped and turned pale. Momentarily the old fire came back to his belly. His chin jutted out. He attempted to barrel his hollow chest. Trying, like a puffer fish, to appear considerably larger than the pathetic shadow he'd become.

"This is a trick," he sneered. "Ye're not fooling me."

John slammed more doors.

Malkie raised his walking stick and shook it in the air.

"Come out, ye damned coward. Show yourself! I'll beat ye to within an inch of your life, so I will."

Johno shivered the timbers.

The walls of the room creaked and trembled.

Fear consumed Malkie's newfound bravado. He seemed so old and vulnerable that Johno almost pitied him. His upper lip trembled over his gap-toothed mouth. His hand shook as he gripped the doorknob and pushed the door open.

Johno slammed it violently back in his face, breaking his nose. Malkie coughed and spat blood. He staggered to the window and tried to open it. Johno brought the sash down hard, shattering his fingers. Malkie leaned heavily on his stick with his left hand, broken right hand dangling limply at his side, blood from his nose staining his shirt. He addressed the name carved into the door panel.

"I'm sorry for what I did. Ye've made your point, son. Now let me go. I'm an old man. I'm not well."

But Johno wasn't finished. His point definitely was not made yet. He warped the door and window frame, trapping Malkie inside the room. He popped the doorknob out with such force it slammed like a bullet into Malkie's chest and brought him to his knees. He wheezed gasped for breath, dropping his stick as he clutched his fractured ribs.

"Please," he begged. "Show some mercy."

Johno had no mercy in him to show.

He remembered that head butt in that cold gunnel on that long ago rainy day. He remembered how he had been kicked like a dog as he lay on the wet ground. He remembered how his fingers were crushed under a boot heel and how he had been exiled from his home and family for nothing. For no justifiable reason at all.

He remembered how he had been brought to this house. How the first bullet had felled him. How the silencer had been placed against his skull to deliver the second bullet. How pictures had been taken of his corpse to use an example. For nothing. For no justifiable reason at all.

He remembered everything that had been lost to him.

He remembered the sadistic pleasure Malkie Hamilton had taken throughout it all.

Full of ire and rage, Johno sent splinters of skirting board whooshing like spears through the air. Malkie jerked and jigged as they thumped into his body. He howled from the pain of their entry. Johno shivered the timbers so violently walls cracked, and beams split. A chunk of plaster crashed down from the ceiling, laying Malkie flat.

Now that he had started, Johno could not stop. All the pent-up anger exploded into the wood of the house. The roof collapsed. The chimney tumbled. Bricks in the walls became dislodged. The stairs fell in on themselves. Johno went on trembling and shivering until the entire house came roaring down on Malkie Hamilton, crushing him like the scuttling roach he always was.

And, as the dust settled on the rubble, the essence of John Andrew Mercer, was finally free to dissipate. Vengeance was his. The house no longer entombed him.

Digging Up the Dead

Ed Ahern

The hardest part of digging up the dead is the paperwork. Greedy descendants, stuffy ministers, meddling historical societies, all wanting to make things difficult. Getting final approval from the town or city was the easiest, they just wanted the low rent corpses gone to make way for taxable condos. This cemetery had a bad reputation, which made things easier.

Despite the difficulties, this was my family profession and I'd suffered through until my two crews could begin using backhoes to gouge out graves. The cemetery wasn't quite old enough to be historical, but plenty old enough for caskets and contents to have decomposed.

I stood next to stacks of 2x2x4 foot wooden boxes being offloaded from a tractor trailer. Nice new pine homes for the unearthed. The corpse bits we found would fit snugly into them, with a little cramming. I shifted my feet. The longer I was away from the diggers the more likely it was that they would find and pocket something valuable, like a diamond ring. And I hung onto all the souvenirs.

"Can you guys work a little faster?"

The stoic faces of the truck driver and his helper looked like overcooked oatmeal. They said nothing, just held to their pace. Ten minutes later, boxes stacked, I was able to go back into the cemetery and perch like a vulture as my crews dug. I hadn't asked them for any paperwork when I'd hired them, illegal aliens were less likely to report some of my shortcuts. Like having them sleep on site so I could work them a little longer.

Just then, the tines of the closer backhoe scoop struck metal.

"Hold it, Tomas!" I yelled, loped over to the back hoe and stared. Two boxes, blacker than the dirt around them, were partially exposed. I jumped into the hole for a closer look. The boxes shined silver where the blade had scraped them.

The smaller box could have held a fancy hat, the larger one a midget. *Dumb-assed luck*. "Don't crush them. Set your scoop lower and pick them up with the dirt. Then bring the load over to my shed."

The backhoe operator stared at me with amiable incomprehension, but I was able - with gestures and broken Spanish - to get the boxes picked up and moved. Once at my shed I hosed them down, then took out a pen knife and scratched the bigger box. The soft metal looked like either sterling or coin silver. Either way worth a lot. It was time to get some advice and I made a long distance phone call.

"Bună zuea bunica"

"Speak English, Anton." Her voice had the familiar rasp of too many bad cigarettes.

"Hello, Grandma. I just found two silver boxes- one medium, one large."

"Tell me you haven't opened them."

"Not yet. Over a hundred years old, so no knowledge of the present."

"Good. You're wearing it?"

60

"Of course," I lied.

"Use the gimmick I taught you. It has to be an agreed bargain, even if it's a bad one."

"Okay." We talked about family for a few minutes and hung up.

I left the boxes where they lay and walked over to my camper. It took me almost a half-hour to find the silver medal and chain. I put it on, went back to the shed and took a closer look.

Both boxes had been locked, but the iron locks had rusted through and broke off when I applied a screwdriver. I opened the hat box first and stared at a skull with a brick between its teeth.

Well, hello there. Somebody really didn't like you.

I pried open the bigger box and found the rest of him, legs bent backward and broken at the knee so the body would fit in. A black metal spike stuck up between some ribs and a quick scrape told me it was also probably silver. I sat down for a second to think things through, then got up and checked the cemetery records and grave site map. Somebody had freeloaded, burying the two boxes unmarked between two legitimate graves.

So no records, no heirs to worry about. Found money.

I drove over to the stack of pine boxes, pulled one off and drove it back to the shed.

You're going to get a proper, almost Christian burial, friend, not that you'll like it much.

I pulled the silver spike out and set it aside, then grabbed the rib cage and shoe-horned it into the pine box. The arm and leg bones came loose as I

61

tried to move them and I wound up cramming them along the sides. He'd been a big sucker and when I tried to put the skull in, it wouldn't fit. I pulled out the brick, tossed it aside and crammed the skull into what had been the guy's stomach cavity. Then I picked up the bigger silver box and tipped it so all the little hand and foot bones rolled into the wood casket. As I reached for the lid the bones settled, as if they were getting more comfortable.

In case my new friend turned out to be a dud, he'd have to be given a name and number so he could get reburied. I fired up the computer and went into the listing of stiffs the cemetery had provided. I opened up a line about a third of the way down the list and typed in a bogus entry for John Argentclad.

Requiescat in pace, buddy. And let's make sure of that.

In case my pal didn't requiescat, I took our pick-up truck and two helpers to the town dump and found a nice big chest freezer with the door still on. We brought it back, set it down next to my shack and put John's box inside it. I wrote "Do not Disturb" and "No Toque" a few times on the sides and top. Then I chained up the freezer and set up some noise alarms. Couldn't have John being relocated.

***

Tomas dropped off his backhoe, stone dead, a week later. He'd been looking gaunt and pale for a few days. My pal John had decided to make trouble. I called the cops and suspended work for two days

62

while they went through the site. They questioned me, of course, but there's no known murder method by fluid loss. Not known to them anyway.

When, six mornings later, Cesar came out of his tent looking like he'd pissed all his blood away, I called him over to my shed.

"Come in, Cesar, shut the door behind you."

"Jefe?"

His tone was subservient, but his belligerent eyes gave him away.

"I know what you are and how you suck out our fluids from within, but not what to call you."

There was silence for half a minute, then what had been Cesar shrugged. "You titled my remains, John, that will do."

"A question, please, John, before we get into it. Why are you called a vampire when what you mostly drain is lymph fluid?"

"Lymph fluid? Ah, the body's waterway. Because your kind stopped figuring us out once you knew how to imprison us."

"Okay. John, I released you so you can do exactly what I tell you."

The was-Cesar-now-John took a step toward me, but stopped, staring at the medal on my chest. Even if he could have tried to hurt me, Cesar's wasted body wouldn't be able to do much. His eyes had shifted to hate.

"You think you know me? Run away before I change my mind."

"John, John, all that dirt has muddied your mind. If I pop the brick and silver spike back into your skeleton today and stick you in the silver boxes before dark, you're back to eternal starvation. Do you really want that?"

His eyes shifted. The hate was still there, but I could see intelligence churning. "If you were going to do that you wouldn't tell me. What is it YOU want?"

"Ah. You've had well over a hundred years to get familiar with this cemetery. I'm operating in the blind here. I need to know where the real valuables are buried, which sadly dead ones I should focus in on. If you tell me that I'll put you in a prime feeding location that will last you for a half century."

"I have no need of your help."

"You're such a shitty liar. We both know that you're bound to within a couple hundred yards of where you're buried and that you can only occupy a body after dark. Even if I don't re-imprison you, your coffin is slated to be moved to a remote wooded area where you'll get to occasionally suck out possums. If you help me, I'll put you on a site with a dense population of transient human goulash."

John stared at the medal. "Your people did this to me."

"Not my people. We Romany tend to have a 'live and let kill' attitude. Here's what we're going to do. You get to finish up Cesar, of course, but I can't have you slurping your way through my work crews. Once you've sworn agreement and told me what I need to know, you have to quit feeding for a while."

His reaction was a feral snarl.

"Hear me out. You've just fed twice, after a century-long abstinence. You'll surely be able to handle a year-long feeding break, after which I'll let you loose on a buffet of literally hundreds of us. And I'm pretty sure you won't be detected.

"I cannot trust a Romany."

"I will swear with the oath we cannot name that what I've just told you is true. You just swear by the same oath that the information you give me is true and you promise to dry out for several months. What do you have to lose? If you don't agree I'll just put you back in your silver boxes."

"Who would I be feeding on?"

"Affluent adults who've been well fed and nourished their whole lives."

"Where would you place me?"

"Right here. In a year this will be luxury accommodations with three hundred plus residents. Easy pickings. I'll set you in the foundation hole just before they pour the concrete. But if you can't point out enough gold, silver and jewellery to fill both your boxes, your future is forfeit and you'll be Argent-clad again."

"You won't wear that medal forever. Are you so sure I won't find you?"

"Don't trouble yourself, John. I plan on always staying at least two football fields away."

"I am timeless and vindictive. Do not think to cheat me."

"What I've said is literally true and I'm ready to swear this to you. Shall we proceed to the oath taking?"

65

John nodded Cesar's head. "I seem to have little choice."

I wrote out the terms and conditions and had him read them. Then we swore the oath (I had to refer to a little black grimoire that looks like a child's missal) and we both signed. John's signature looked like crisscrossing runes, but he swore under the oath that it was his native script.

We honored our pact. John didn't suck out any more of the help and after they'd dug the foundation cavity, I snuck in one Sunday afternoon, dug a little deeper, and popped in John's pine box. The next day they poured the concrete on top of him.

The jewelry, mementos and gold and silver netted me almost a half million dollars. John's silver boxes alone got me more than ten thousand.

Six months later the building was ready for occupancy and they started bringing in tenants. In wheelchairs and on gurneys. John hadn't asked and I hadn't told him about who would live there. It was a hospice for the soon to die. John would have to eat his food fast and I was pretty sure that with all their decay, disease and drugs, the terminally ill would taste terrible. I had put John in culinary purgatory, suffering if he starved, repulsed if he ate. I do like tidy solutions.

Leitmotif

Paul Edwards

"Sounds – possibly musical – heard in the night from other worlds or realms of being."
- H.P. Lovecraft

Viktor was woken by the sound of soft, sweet music.

He lay there listening, hands clasped across his chest, fingers intertwined.

The music filled his head with an assortment of images:

Magic circles chalked on stripped bare floorboards. Scattered scraps of hand drawn sheet music. A photograph of a smiling couple in a frame propped up on the lid of a grand piano. A dusty bookcase crammed with esoteric tomes and crumbling grimoires.

Darkness tugged at the corners of his vision. He was having trouble keeping his eyes open. Sleep was pulling him back in its full embrace. But the music was haunting, almost impossible to tune out of, its magic brushing away his lethargy and suffusing him with joy.

His arms dropped to his sides, his fingers lightly tapping the base of the bed. The music, he realised, was coming from a lone violin. This unlocked precious memories within him, each one startlingly vivid and emotional in detail.

They helped draw him to his feet at last, the bones in his body popping. He edged across the room, pressing his hands up against the door. The door yielded, creaking quietly open.

Beyond the door stood a woman, her eyelids fluttering, a baroque violin tucked under her chin. Moonlight glinted off the necklace she wore: a large silver pentacle attached to a chain. Long grey hair with black roots fell about her face as she shimmied and swayed, a discarded padlock lying on the ground between her feet.

She lifted her head, catching his gaze.

Immediately, her eyes widened.

Her jaw dropped.

She played on, the melody painting the night and the insides of his skull with wonder.

She was smiling and crying, all at the same time.

And then he remembered.

It was *his* song.

The song Ilse had written.

Ilse, he thought; *of course!*

The song that spoke of a special bond, stronger than any obstacle, than any adversary. And *he* was the song – it was part of his essence, his very being intertwined with the sparse, ghostly refrain.

Her black lace dress swished about her ankles, tears leaking down her aged but still breathtakingly beautiful face.

When the music stops, he thought, *sleep will steal me from the world once more.*

But for now, he remained entranced in the doorway of his small stone house, watching,

listening to her play his song amongst the crosses
and headstones of the garden.

Year of the Cat

Rickey Rivers Jr.

On the way home I ran into a cat. The cat followed me home. It seemed hungry so I gave it some food. I guess it's mine now. I went on the internet to look for names until I decided on one: Terra.

Terra's cute with white fur and dark eyes. I was surprised at how clean her fur was considering she was a stray. She kept herself clean, I guess. She's good company too, as much good company as a cat can be. I think I'll keep her around.

***

I took Terra to the vet to get her shots. She was quiet the whole time. Even the vet was surprised.

"Such a good kitty…"

I said thanks like I played a part in that. In a way I guess I did. Every living creature needs food and a home.

***

Terra's an inside cat, but recently she's been getting out and into the neighbor's yards. I've disciplined her as best you can discipline a cat. I don't like the word discipline, but that's what it was.

I've fed her a little less, yelled at her. Maybe that'll teach her a lesson. I felt bad about doing that.

***

Terra seems better behaved now. I love her. I don't know why, but there's something about her specifically. She's soft, fluffy and kind to me. She doesn't make much noise.

***

I had company over, but they had to leave sooner than they wanted to. Terra doesn't like other people. I'll have to monitor that. I hope the neighborhood strays haven't had a negative effect on her. Peer pressure works with animals too and stray cats are often dirty.

***

Terra bit me. I'm taking her back to the vet soon to see if she's has rabies or something.

***

Terra won't let me get her into her cage. I guess we're not going to the vet. She's been aggressive lately. I'm not sure what's wrong. She's been eating other things besides food. It worries me. I called an in-house vet.

***

71

Terra went after the in-house vet. I tried to call the pound, but Terra ran after me when I got near the phone. I'm in the bathroom now, I'm bleeding. Glad I keep the first aid kit in here. I hear her running around and scratching against the door. She's mad at me. She's clawing the door handle.

***

Terra left. I got out of the bathroom and saw a hole in the living room window. The furniture was flipped over. My coffee table was broken.

***

I boarded up the window Terra escaped from. She won't be able to get in again. That's a shame, but not really. I don't think I want her anymore.

A few stray cats have started hanging around the house. They must know someone was feeding strays over here. But I was only feeding one, I'm not feeding strays anymore. All of these new cats look like Terra to me. I've counted four.

***

I called the in-house vet again. She didn't want to come out. I called the pound, but there was static on the other end. It must be a holiday or some special day, either that or the person who was supposed to pick up just couldn't pick up for some reason. I called five times. When I called another location I thought I heard a long meow, but it sounded like a person.

I saw nine white Terra-like cats today. I was scared to go outside. I called into work. I said I was sick.

***

They got in.

***

I'll have to see what to do with them. They're so quiet. They're almost not even here. If you closed your eyes you couldn't tell. But I won't close my eyes for too long. I can't.

***

I have to feed them. So I'm feeding them. I don't have much to give, but I'm feeding them.

***

I've apologized, but they don't understand, or they choose not to understand. And they're still feeding, and quiet, so quiet and hungry, so hungry.

Tips

Diane Arrelle

I guess the first time I noticed all was not well in the world was when a Zombie ate my dog.

Actually, having Muffy devoured by a mindless animated corpse wasn't the end of the world for me. The nasty dog had belonged to my late husband, Henry. What did disturb me was that it was my late husband munching on the mutt.

I stood rooted in the doorway as my deceased spouse chewed Muffy's legs off. I mean, Henry was never a drumstick kind of guy.

Henry was covered in dirt and I could smell him clear across the yard. I fought off the urge to call him, after all, I'd seen the zombie movies and knew what fate awaited anyone who got near them. So, I closed and locked the back door and, with mixed emotions, realized I never had to refill the dog bowl again.

I sat in the kitchen, wishing the acid jumping up my throat would settle down. I may not have liked the dog but I hadn't wanted it dead and certainly not shredded and eaten by its master.

And the thought I had avoided finally broke through. *Why was Henry a zombie*?

As if in answer, I became aware of pandemonium from outside: screams, cars crashing, gun shots. I turned on the television. The first 676 stations I turned to consisted of reruns, infomercials, movies, gameshows, soaps, talkshows, cooking shows, exercise shows and evangelists screaming to their god for salvation and to their audience for money.

Finally I found a local news station. I saw pretty newscasters describing the scenes, showing videos of zombies in varying states of decay stumbling around. I watched the tube hoping for guidance, but none came. Instead the phone rang. I picked it up and heard my boss, Louie, yelling.

"Rita! Where are you?" he bellowed. "You were due in half an hour ago!"

I wondered if he was totally mad. "Uh, Louie, didn't you notice that the world seems to be ending? There are zombies outside."

"So?" he yelled. "That means you get a day off? I don't think so. Get in here by 11:00 for the lunch crowd."

"Lou, do you really think anyone will be in for lunch?"

"Of course, the specials are beef stew or meatball subs, both big sellers!"

I sighed, "I'll try, but if I get eaten by a zombie, you're the first one I'll come after."

He laughed. "Rita, how can you get eaten by a zombie? They're brain dead for Chrissake. If one comes at you, walk around it."

He made sense. I went out as soon as the coast was clear. Lou was right, zombies can't really think and since they are in various stages of rot, they can't move very fast. Not two blocks from my rowhouse, I saw a pair of them, a man dragging his leg and stumbling and a woman right behind him with her dress shredded and the flesh on her torso pretty much eaten away. They groaned incoherently, lifted their arms like sleepwalkers and started for me.

My stomach clenched and I swear I felt my blood heat drop several degrees. I froze, I couldn't think, I couldn't breathe. They were going to get me. Then, just as suddenly as I froze up, the adrenaline kicked in, filling me up with internal fire. So I crossed the street.

I walked briskly away and, although they tried to follow, I let them eat my dust. After that, whenever I saw a zombie, I just gave it space and it just shuffled on like I didn't exist.

I walked twelve blocks to work and wondered how much thinking they could do with their brains filled with embalming fluids and pretty much the consistency of bread pudding.

Lou was correct, much to my utter shock. Customers were filing in and filling all the booths and counter seats. Only it wasn't for the beef, it was the human need to huddle together in the dark. The world was suddenly all wrong and people needed to congregate and talk. Even though I hustled for three hours straight serving platters and filling endless coffee cups, the conversations made the time fly.

During the noon broadcast, the media finally realized that the world was in a state of crisis. The newscasters had tons of experts with expert opinions on exactly what was happening and why we suddenly had zombies in our midst. The expert testimonies varied from toxic waste, to aliens, to Armageddon, but the one thing everyone agreed on was that zombies were fictional monsters and impossible in the real world. They were dead. Dead cannot rise mindless and attack the living. The only experts to express a different opinion were featured on the SciFi Channel which then followed with a "B" zombie movie marathon.

The next day the news was even bleaker. The zombies were starting to travel in packs and the newly dead were a lot quicker than their rotting companions. They were attacking people: individuals walking alone, street dwellers, old-age centers and of course, teenagers who insisted they were invincible and ignored the warnings.

I gave up worrying about the world and wondered if I needed to pay my mortgage. Just in case the material world survived, I went to work, only I drove my old car that had been sitting in the driveway ever since gas prices went up. Just as I figured, parking was no problem.

I went in and looked at Lou and the two customers sipping coffee. "So, you think the rush is over for today?" I asked. "Looks like tips are going to be light."

Louie just shrugged and watched the television. I followed his gaze. The zombies were growing in numbers, there was the usual rioting and looting and of course everyone suddenly rediscovering their religion.

Only a few people wandered in, although one guy came in waving a gun. He looked around quickly then screamed at Louie. "All your money! Now!"

Louie didn't even bat an eye. He reached toward the register and asked, "Whatcha need the money for, to pay the zombies for protection?"

The punk's face went ashen. "Uh, no, don't need nothin'," and he backed out the door.

I turned to look at Louie and saw him holding a shotgun. "Puts his popgun to shame, don't it?" he said conversationally, turning back toward the television. "Picked it up in case. Won't kill a zombie, but it sure will slow the sucker down if I blow off its leg."

I nodded and glanced over at the only customer in the place cowering in the last booth. "It's OK, Dave, you can get up now."

Dave stood and tried to act dignified, although it had to be difficult since he had to get out from under the table and his pants were wet. "That would make a great story, Lou," he said and took out his skinny reporter's notepad. "Can get you on the morning edition's front page."

Louie warmed to the idea immediately. He turned to Dave and hit off on the remote. "OK, ask away, buddy, and for you, the coffee's free."

Overnight, Louie became a star... hero to the living, who swamped the place because, even facing what seemed to be the end of the world, people love celebrity.

After a month or so, the customers started dwindling and the numbers of zombies began to increase. It soon became obvious that the older, rotting zombies were falling apart, leaving pieces and limbs all over the streets. Their brains had turned from pudding to sludge that dribbled out of the openings in their heads.

Life was actually back to a routine; only the mean streets were a little more dangerous. People carried weapons, guns and gasoline soaked torches, because, while most of the zombie myths turned out to be pure fiction, setting the living dead on fire prove to be a sure way to make them permanently dead.

Most of the original zombies had gone, rotted away, but the new zombies, the ones who had been alive when they were turned, well, they were never really dead and they still weren't, at least not totally. They had that blank-faced stare, moaned and slobbered, but their limbs stayed intact, their eyes weren't turning to gooey marbles, they had most of their coordination and worst of all, speed. If they ever figured out how to band together as a thinking cohesive unit, mankind would be doomed.

I drove to work every day because I felt safer around Lou and the few regulars that still came in. Then it happened. One day after the breakfast crowd, a word I use loosely, the door opened and in came three zombies. They stood by the door and did nothing. One looked confused, then pained. "Huuuuh," he said and pointed at the counter.

"Give 'em a menu!" Lou whispered.

I stayed behind the counter.

Lou grunted with disgust, walked over to the undead trio and held the cardboard menus out like a peace offering. The man who had made the sound slapped them away. Lou backed up a step, just out of biting range and said to me, "Set up three coffees and butter some of that leftover toast."

I started at him like he was mad. I mean he had to be mad to even suggest feeding zombies.

"Do it!"

I did, I don't remember ever taking my eyes off the living dead customers, but somehow there were three set-ups with fresh coffee and toast. I pointed at the counter and to my shock, the small group walked slowly over and after many attempts to sit on the stools, they remained seated and upright. The moaner turned his dull eyes toward me and said, "Huuuuuh." Then he picked up the coffee cup with both hands and spilled it down his front. The other two followed his example and then picked up the toast. The one in the middle, a rotting woman, shoved the buttered triangle into her cheek, tearing a hole in the soft, unresilient flesh. The other man managed at get some into his mouth and stopped dead. His features twisted into the most awful thing I think I had ever seen. Repulsed, I stepped farther away.

"MMMMM" he managed after a few tries. I stared at the spray of crumbs that had spilled out of his opened mouth and with a shudder; I realized he was trying to smile.

"Good, good," Lou said and smiled back, "See?" he said, turning to me. "Business is picking up!"

I watched as the three struggled to get out of their seats. "Business? Business?" I screamed. "They're dead, for the love of anything holy. What do you think, that they'll pay you? God, Lou, I can't go on like this, dead people are becoming our best customers, I'm broke, haven't made a decent tip in weeks, ever since this began and you say business is picking up?"

Lou shrugged, "Baby, you just need to be adaptable."

Dave got up from behind the pinball machine, "Wow! What a story...Diner for the Undead! Bet I make front page."

Lou beamed. "Somehow I'm going to get rich off of all this publicity. I can feel it in my bones. Rita, didn't I tell you the world wasn't coming to an end, just a new beginning?"

The next day, the luncheonette made the front page. Lou sat and admired the headline, then five zombies entered the diner and headed for the counter. The original three and two buddies. I quickly got out the coffees and toast and Lou shouted to pick up an abandoned order of pancakes.

The zombies moaned and grunted like they were in dead pig heaven. When they finished, they shuffled off to do whatever it was that zombies do.

Each day the zombies came, five then six, then they started coming in separate groups. We fed them, after all a sated zombie was not a hungry zombie and as the days progressed, attacks on the living in the blocks around the eatery fell off.

It was a Saturday, not that the days counted for anything anymore. A group of four zombies had just sat down to plates of day old tuna salad when Dave left his booth and walked up behind them.

He tapped one on the shoulder. "Say," he began. "Can you guys speak at all? I'd like to —"

Before he could finish the sentence, the zombie turned and sank his teeth in Dave's head, ripping off a huge chuck. Dave cried out and fell to the floor, silent and still as the blood pooled around him.

I turned, threw up, then sank to my knees and cried. I didn't get up again until the zombies who had returned to their meal got up and left.

I looked over the counter. Lou was nudging Dave with his toe. "Guess that ends the free publicity," he sighed and dragged Dave's body to the curb. Then he came back in and called the zombie victim hotline. "Got a corpse on the curb," he said and gave the address.

I didn't stay to see if the torch squad came and incinerated Dave, I just left and went home to my safe boarded up house. I stayed locked inside a few days, but the walls just seemed to close in on me. With no place else to go, I went into work on the fourth day.

Lou watched me enter and never said a word. After a few minutes the zombies started wandering in. Some things had changed in the time I took off. When they finished eating, one of the zombies got up and carried the dishes into the kitchen. Another got up and swept the floor.

Lou smiled. "They just started working for their food. It seems that perhaps there is still a little humanity left in them or else maybe they are just evolving."

"Evolving," I snapped. "They're freaking dead, Lou!"

82

Dave came shuffling in; obviously the torchers hadn't come for him in time. He sat, trying to eat, but he was still getting the hang of being reanimated. He smiled at me and said "Huuiii Riiiiitaahhh"

My mouth dropped open.

Lou's smile broadened. "Like I said, a new generation, a little smarter. Evolution!"

The Zombie who had taken that first bite of toast all those days ago finished eating, turned to stare at me with those dull, lifeless eyes and gave me a god-awful smile. "TPPPPPPPPPP" he sort of gurgled and pointed at a hand he left on the counter next to the plate.

I wanted to scream, then I noticed a diamond ring on one of the gray, bloated fingers.

"Tppppppppppppp!"

I nodded at my first tip in weeks and tried to smile back at my customer. Evolution happens in many ways, I decided, as I pried the ring off the hand.

Home

Paul Edwards

Mum and Carl were in the kitchen, talking to somebody I didn't recognise. The official was tall and lean, with a tanned, tear-shaped face. An ID card displaying a miniaturised version of that same face hung around his neck, crocodile-clipped to a lanyard.

"Once a year," he said, "the veil between worlds wears so thin that…"

I withdrew into the lounge, fixing my gaze on the wingback chair by the window. Sometimes I can still picture Dad there, smoking and drinking neat whisky, black threads from his cigarette coiling upwards, upwards.

A blur of movement snapped me from my thoughts. I looked up to see Will, dressed in faded jeans and a hoodie, crossing the road outside the window.

The kitchen door squeaked as it widened, the man declaring, "…about fear, or *controlling* it. That's what he'll feed on. That's what he wants from you all."

I edged back into the hall, my hands crushed together in front of me.

"The first time is always the worst," the man said, stepping out of the kitchen with a small suitcase in his hand. "And I can tell it's been hanging over you all for some time. Don't let it spoil the good you have here." He nodded at me. "She's worth fighting for. They both are."

He left us at last, closing the front door behind him, me, Mum and Carl taking ourselves off into the stillness and quiet of the lounge.

Mum was silent for a while. Then, following my gaze to our father's chair, she put her hands on her hips and said, "Can't believe how stupid I've been. I should've made the room less familiar for him."

Carl grabbed hold of the chair, turning it and pushing it away into the corner of the room. "When we've got the money," he said, straightening, smiling weakly, "we'll replace it. About time we had a refurbish, right?"

I know Carl makes Mum feel safe. Makes us all feel safe, I suppose. He doesn't have to be here, not really. Someday I hope to feel comfortable enough to call him Dad.

"Where's Will?" Mum asked us, a sudden tinge of fear in her voice. "It's getting late. He should be home by now."

She looked at me and I shrugged, not letting on that I'd seen him just now. "Don't worry," I said, snatching my coat from off the back of the sofa. "I'll find him."

"Be careful." Panic flashed through her eyes. "You can say the man's gone, if that's what's been bothering him."

I opened the door and hurried outside, streetlamps winking on around me. I shoved my hands in my pockets, stalking the lanes and back alleys of the estate, calling his name. Between blocks of mouldering terraces, I watched the sunset spread its fire across town.

Clustered in a black doorway was a family of four—father, mother, son and daughter—their faces powdered white and their eyes rimmed with kohl. They smiled at me as I passed. There was a banner reading WELCOME HOME taped to the brickwork above their heads. Tea-lights burned on the windowsill, positioned between gaudy papier-mâché skulls, charms and other esoteric trinkets.

I quickened my pace, food packets and wrappers blowing about my ankles. I leapt over a crumbling stone wall and crouched amongst briars and weeds, a crooked spire cutting into the sky above.

Between skewed black railings I saw his face through twilight's cold, accreting layers. There were others here, too, but they kept separate vigils; waiting and watching, they wanted to be the first to greet their dead.

I unlatched the gate, stepping around it and entering the graveyard. Will was sitting at Dad's grave, a wicked looking knife on his lap.

I crouched by his side. "Come home," I breathed.

"Home?" His gaze lifted and focused on the granite slab which bore our father's name. "Nowhere's home, Sylvie."

I noticed his hands were clenched, his brows knotted together. I reached out, gently shaking him. "Hate won't change a thing. Remember what the man said?"

"Fuck the suits and the social workers," he hissed. "*They* can't stop him from coming."

I managed to shape my mouth into a smile. "But *we* need you. And if we're going to get through this…" I paused mid-sentence and watched the tears leak down his face.

"I *look* like him, Sylvie. I share his fucking DNA."

"You're *nothing* like him." I took hold of his face, turning him toward me. "You don't have his eyes, right? Look—you have Mum's eyes. You're not like him at all."

"But he always knew how to get inside me." He shoved me away, wiping the tears from his cheeks with the sleeve of his hoodie. "Remember Benji?"

A year ago, when Dad was still alive, Will'd smashed a bottle of whisky; in retaliation, Dad killed our pet dog by stringing it up by its neck with the belt he used to hit us with.

"Will." I touched his hand and his face screwed up into a grimace. "I hate him, too. The nights I lay there, scared, waiting for…"

"I should've known," he spat. "Should have realised. I could have stopped…"

"None of it's *your* fault." I wrapped my arm around his shoulders. "What matters is you're here *now*. For me. Mum, too."

"But I'm frightened about what he can do. *Still* do."

"You're strong, Will…"

"I'm not strong, Sylvie." He shoved me again and clambered to his feet, collecting up his knife.

87

Together, we staggered out of the graveyard and made our way homewards.

Mum met us at the front door. "You're back," she gasped. "Thank God you're back." Will managed to conceal his knife from her beneath the front of his hoodie sweatshirt. In the lounge, Carl was standing by the window, peering out at people gathering in the street, lanterns and candle flames bobbing like will-o'-the-wisps in the darkness.

Mum sucked in a breath. "I'll make a start on supper, eh?"

Will dashed upstairs before anyone could stop him.

"Will!" Mum cried. "*Please*. We should..."

Carl seized her arm. "It's enough that he's here. Let him be, love."

Mum nodded, perched herself on the sofa, and quietly muttered, "Suppose all we can do now is wait."

Carl pulled the curtains along their runners, screening the outside world from view. I paced the room, thoughts all over the place. Moments later, I went upstairs to check on Will.

His bedroom door was ajar and I peered curiously into the gloom, seeing him sat at the foot of his bed with the knife still on his lap. I knocked, calling out his name. He looked up and around, shadows falling across his face.

"I *want* him real," he growled. "I want to hurt him, Sylvie."

"But that'll give him what he wants, remember?"

88

He swore under his breath, leapt to his feet and closed the door in my face, leaving me all alone on the landing.

Down in the kitchen, Mum had pulled on her grey, woollen cardigan. "It's gotten really cold in here," she said. She shifted on her stool and held her hands out to me, and I sat on her lap, letting her pull me in close. "If you hear him," she whispered, "don't listen to a word he says. Don't give him the satisfaction, okay?"

Carl switched the radio on, but it immediately turned itself off again. He glanced around, confusion stamped across his features. I pretended it hadn't happened, pressing my ear to Mum's chest instead, tuning in to the sound of her rapidly accelerating heartbeat.

I felt a hand on my shoulder, stubble scraping my cheek.

"Promise we'll be alone again soon, Sylvie."

I shrieked and recoiled, Mum enveloping me with her arms, holding and squeezing me tight. I was gasping and shaking, aware of the stench of whisky and cigarette smoke carrying in the air.

"He's here," I cried. "He was right beside me!"

Will charged downstairs, his eyes wide and startled looking. We met him in the lounge just as our father's chair scraped across the floor toward us.

Dad's face began to form, white and luminous, flickering, sneering above the wingback chair.

Will saw it and immediately pulled the knife from behind his back.

"No." I stepped forward, putting my hand on Will's arm.

The leering visage wavered and shimmered, surrounded by flickering wisps of ethereal fog.

Carl seized Will's shoulders, turning him, steering him out the room and into the hall. "It won't do a thing, Will," he whispered. Will's head was lowered, his breathing ragged and uneven sounding. It wasn't just Will—we were all scared; thoughts of this night and what it might bring have been gnawing away at us for months.

I raised my head to see Dad sink into his chair, an awful grin materialising on his face. He looked like he was composed of mist, his body swirling and reconstituting every time he moved. He opened his mouth, emitting brays of horrible, echoey laughter.

"Go away," I snarled. *Fuck off and leave us alone. We're not leaving because of you. Not tonight, not* ever.

Me and Mum clutched at each other, trying to show him we were strong, that he couldn't break us. We closed our eyes, not wanting to see him, to even acknowledge his presence. The ensuing minutes felt like hours. *You're not here,* I kept thinking. *There's only me, Mum, Will and Carl. We're family. A force to be reckoned with.*

Eventually a kind of stillness, a wave of peace, descended and we reopened our eyes, our bodies sweating despite the cold.

"Is he…?" Mum glanced around, eyes drawn to the wingback chair once more. She shivered and wrapped her arms around herself. Will shuffled back into the room, the knife gone and his gaze nailed to the floor. He still looked so pale and jittery, I thought.

We could hear whoops and shouting coming from the street, but it was different here. Was always going to be, I suppose.

Had he *really* passed through?

My heart rate began to slow and I felt much less anxious, much less afraid.

Will made for the stairs.

"Will…" Mum said, her head snapping up. *"Stay. Please."*

"It's okay." He tried placating her with a smile. "He's gone. He must have. Everything's normal again, right?"

Carl was by Mum's side now, gripping her hand, stroking her knuckles with his fingers. Mum watched Will traipse upstairs, her expression telling me she was still concerned about him.

I perched on the sofa, listening to the hollers, shrieks and cheers coming from the celebrants outside. It sounded all so alienating, all so unreal.

Mum and Carl retired to the kitchen to make coffee. The temperature felt normal, the house still again.

I rose, making for the stairs.

"Sylvie?" Mum called.

"Just checking on Will," I said.

"Ask him to come down, love."

I found him in the bathroom, squinting and staring at his features in the mirror above the sink. *I look like him.*

It was bright in there, the strip light casting its stark luminescence onto his face. By his sides, his hands were screwed up into tight, trembling balls. "Will?"

His eyes rolled in my direction, his countenance flickering, as if another face was trying to overlay itself on top.

I stepped back, startled. He lunged around me, closing the door before I could flee. His eyes were a different colour, I realised. Cigarette smoke and whisky fumes rode on his breath.

"Promised we'd be alone again," he hissed and, as Will's anguished, screaming features appeared and then disappeared, his hands unclenched and reached for me.

D for Dancing

Rickey Rivers Jr.

Momma and I were sitting in the living room. I was on the floor and she was in her chair looking out the window. It was summer time and the cicadas were singing. It was peaceful, the kind of peace you don't appreciate until you're older.

At some point Momma spoke to herself. She said, "I wonder where he's going?"

I left my toys and joined her at the window. There was a man walking on the dirt road towards the house. He wasn't close, but recognizable.

"Who's that, Momma?" I said.

"That's… Mr. Mason," she said.

I remembered him. He was always a nice man. Mr. Mason used to help my Momma outside with the vegetables. Momma always said he had a strong back and kind eyes. I didn't understand why he stopped coming around. He and Momma seemed to get along well. I liked him too. He used to sing songs while he worked.

I went to the front door to greet him but Momma stopped me.

"Don't you move," said Momma.

I stopped. My hand was maybe an inch from the doorknob. I was dressed. I had on shoes. So what was wrong?

"Strange," said Momma, "how very strange."

She was talking to herself again with a serious look on her face. Meanwhile, Mr. Mason was getting closer and closer to the house.

I went back to her and once again looked outside. Mr. Mason was dancing now, a funny kind of dance, back and forth, in our direction, saunter-like and smooth. He seemed light on his feet, like he danced on air. The dance made me smile. I wanted to join him. He looked like he was having fun.

"Momma," I said. "Can I dance with him?"

Momma didn't say anything. She kept her eyes on him. Her nostrils flared and sweat trickled down her neck.

Mr. Mason continued to dance and move in a silent rhythm towards the house, his dark suit moving in the breeze, his white shirt bright in the sun. He reminded me of a marionette. He was always as thin as one.

"Very strange indeed," said Momma.

"What's so strange?" I asked.

Mr. Mason had almost reached our front porch when Momma stood up and went to the front door. She snatched it open and stood in the doorway. "Go back!" she yelled. "We don't want any trouble."

I stood there staring at her. She was always so nice to him before and he was always so nice to the both of us. So why was she yelling at him now? She only yelled when she was angry. And she couldn't be angry with him. He hadn't been around in a while. I thought to myself, maybe that's why she's mad, because he stopped coming around?

Still she went on. "Mr. Mason, YOU ARE NOT WELCOME HERE!"

Her voice was shaky. She didn't sound like herself. It scared me. Mr. Mason didn't deserve to be screamed at. Regardless, slowly but surely I saw him stop, turn and dance away from us. Now he moved in a kind of sad manner. I felt bad for him.

"Momma," I said. "That was rude."

She didn't say anything. She just shut the door, went back to her chair and sat back down. She wiped her sweat and kept looking outside. At some point she began to hum to herself, an old gospel song. She had always done this when she got upset or stressed. She said it calmed her nerves.

"I wanted to dance with him," I said.

But Momma just hummed, keeping her gaze on Mr. Mason. It was like she wasn't there, not all the way.

Finally I said, "I never knew Mr. Mason could dance like that."

Momma looked at me and laughed, "He was always a good dancer."

"A good singer too," I said.

"Yeah," said Momma. "I would have let you go out there too, if he were still alive."

I felt a funny feeling inside, like my heart was bouncing around my stomach. I swear the cicadas went quiet and hid inside of me.

I stood there looking at Momma then asked if I could go on the porch. My head was heavy. She said yes, but not to follow him. I went out. I didn't follow him, but I was looking. Mr. Mason was like midnight in broad daylight. A man-shaped dot becoming smaller and smaller, dancing, all the way back to his grave.

Dead Man's Pond

Rie Sheridan Rose

Jeremy crouched behind a stump, panting from exhaustion, trying desperately to silence the ragged gasps. Suddenly his head went up like an alert stag and—with a muffled sob—he stumbled on.

He ran and ran, the breath ripping from his lungs in painful rasps. Every few yards he glanced back over his shoulder, then spurred forward. When his attention was distracted, he caught his foot on a tree root and slammed into the ground, striking his head against a rock. He tried to get his arms beneath him to push to his feet, but fell back, unconscious....

One bright spring morning, with the birds twittering invitingly from the canopy of the wood and the sun smiling down in conspiratorial splendor, Jeremy Pendleton decided to play a little hooky and go fishing.

I'll catch it from Mom when I get home, but it's worth it not to be cooped up in school on a great day like today. He snatched up his fishing gear and backpack and headed out the door.

The air was cool and smelled of growing things. School smelt like gym socks and pine cleanser.

Besides, we were three months ahead of them in California. I've done all this stuff before. It won't kill me to miss a day.

There was a quiet little pool right in the middle of the wood where you could catch the prettiest trout to be found anywhere in the county. Jeremy took his pole to this spot as soon as his mother's car had pulled out of the drive. He was responsible for getting himself to the bus stop on time since she had to be clocked in well before the bus arrived. Today he just conveniently *forgot*… and went fishing.

Jeremy was crazy for fishing. Since he could first stick a worm on a hook, he'd spent every spare dime on tackle and bait. His father had been a commercial fisherman before Jeremy was born and he'd taught his son a love of the sport that survived the dissolution of his marriage.

The boy had been to the little pond many times before in the six weeks they'd lived here and the fish were always biting. Today, however, he didn't have a single strike.

He decided to try a new place, one he and Billy Standish had seen the week before. Billy had said the new place was haunted and no sensible fellow would go there—especially not near dark.

Jeremy had laughed off Billy's fears, being the sophisticate from California and not brought up on Kentucky superstition.

But I gotta admit it's a little spooky back in here, he confessed to himself as he walked through the darkening trees. *Mom'll be getting off work soon, she'll suspect something is*… he smirked to himself… *fishy if I'm not there when she gets home.*

97

But I can't quit with nothing to show for the whole day.

He shrugged off his unease and stepped through a fringe of underbrush into the tiny clearing. He forgot his misgivings—and the time—in a lively bout of fishing which soon netted him a full stringer.

The fish almost seem eager to leave the pool. He grinned at the fancy.

When Jeremy glanced up at last, he noticed to his dismay that the sun was beginning to slip down behind the trees. He glanced down at his watch. *Geez, I'll never make it home before dark. And Mom'll be home in twenty minutes.*

I'd better camp out tonight and go home tomorrow. I'd just get lost if I tried to navigate these woods at night.

It's a good thing it's Friday. Mom'll kill me in the morning. Still, I'd better call and leave her a message. She knows I can take care of myself, so I doubt she'll worry too much... but I don't think she's gonna like what I did all day long either.

Jeremy was accustomed to roaming alone and always went prepared for any eventuality. He pulled his cell phone out of his jacket and saw the battery was nearly dead. *Great genius. Couldn't remember to plug the darn thing in, now could you? Maybe it's got one call left in it.*

He hit the button for home and when it connected, spoke rapidly to the answering machine. "Hi, Mom. Went fishing and forgot the time. Camping overnight. Don't—"

The cell phone beeped and went dead in his hand. *Well, at least that got most of the details across.*

Jeremy surveyed the clearing with a practiced eye, then swept clear a patch of dirt to build a fire. He'd been an Eagle Scout back home in civilization. Best outdoorsman in his troop. The patented tepee of sticks was soon assembled in his makeshift fire pit, then he pulled a lighter from his pocket and had the campfire blazing. The scent of sizzling fish rose with the smoke and Jeremy filled the mug he kept in his backpack. The water was clear, cold and surprisingly sweet. Cooked fish and fresh water made for a fine supper and before long he felt full and lazy.

This is the life. You can't do stuff like this back home. Mom would have had a cow if I'd tried to stay out all night in California... but I am fifteen. I'm glad we came here, even if no one's got cable and the nearest mall's fifty miles away.

He watched the fire die down to a nest of glowing embers, his eyelids drifting closed at shorter and shorter intervals each time he forced them open. Finally, they stayed shut and he fell into a light doze until midnight.

Suddenly he jerked awake—every nerve tingling as if he had stuck a finger in a light socket. Alert to any unfamiliar movement, Jeremy rose to a crouch and scanned the silent glade. His gaze traveled around the clearing, starting on his left and making it halfway around the glen before he shrank against the tree behind him with a strangled cry.

Directly across the pool were three indistinct figures in black, their faces dimly highlighted by the moon at their backs. Jeremy cowered against the tree as one of the figures spoke in a voice like wind in reeds, "Don't you worry none, boy. We just want to play a game with you. You's the fust one as been here in a long time. We never gets to play with no one ever comin' here no more."

"Yes, boy," chimed in a second shape, "come play with us. We play fine games down in the water, but no one plays with us but the slimy ol' fishes. We wants someone warm to play down there with us."

The figures moved closer... hollow-eyes women with fish-pale skin and long, waving black hair dripping with water. Their clothes were rotting black shrouds spilling moist rivulets to the floor of the clearing and they glided rather than walked.

"He's a fishering man, he is," gloated the first speaker. "He should like our games."

"Aye," replied the second, reaching out bony fingers, "we knows much to do with fishes."

Jeremy felt his dinner threatening to crawl back up his gullet. He scrambled away on his hands and butt, afraid to take his eyes from them, backing into a tree. He could retreat no further.

He was in the presence of some unspeakable danger. Jeremy pushed against the tree, needing to flee the clearing. Something invisible seemed to root him in place.

He covered his ears with his hands as the third figure began to speak. Its voice was a hollow, ringing boom that struck terror to his very soul.

"Come to us, child. You cannot escape us forever. You've drunk of our water; you've eaten our fish; you belong to us now. Sooner or later you will be our plaything. Come to us! We weary of this game."

The figure gestured and Jeremy found himself moving forward against his will. His mind reeled in horror even as his body moved without his control.

Jeremy gathered all the resources of his California soul—of his world where Play Station II was more influence than tales around the campfire and heroes always won—he shouted his defiance. "Never!"

The denial broke the spell and he spun on his heel, racing from the clearing. Behind him he could hear cries of consternation and anger. There was a high, ululating scream and then he felt rather than saw the three spirits following him.

Borne on the wind were shrieks of "Play, boy! Come back and play!"

Jeremy sobbed and ran faster, his hands and face whipped by razor-thin branches, the smell of fear rank in his nostrils. He sped on until he was ready to drop in his tracks and he stumbled as he ran.

I've got to rest!

Jeremy crouched behind a stump, panting from exhaustion, hands cupped around mouth in a desperate attempt to silence the ragged gasps. His head went up like a stag testing the wind, and—with a muffled sob—he stumbled on, breath ripping from his lungs in painful rasps.

Just once he looked back, caught his foot on a tree root and sprawled to the ground, The blackness flooded over him.

When he came to his senses, he remembered where he was. *I've got to get out of here before they catch me!*

He tried to stand, but froze when he saw the phantoms in a semi-circle not five feet beyond him. He fell to his knees, defeated.

The third figure began to speak once more, its voice like black ice, "Running is of no avail. We can follow forever. You disturbed our peace and now you must pay the cost."

It reached across and grabbed Jeremy's arm. He cried out at the pain of the icy touch. The other shades converged upon him. He felt touches of their slime-covered fingers, heard whispering and cackling as they toyed with his clothes and hair. Jeremy refused to process this input—so alien to his twenty-first century soul—and the next thing he realized was he had been returned to the sheltered pond.

"It is time," intoned the lead figure and Jeremy found fighting to be of no use. They dragged him toward the beckoning water.

"Please! Let me go. Let me go!" he screamed, the last word a rising wail of sound.

"We just want to play with you, boy…"

And the cold caressing waters closed over his head.

Anyone foolish enough to pass within sight of that glade hears evil laughter and the sound of terrified cries filling the air with pleas and protests. And if the passer-by steps closer—his cat-like curiosity engaged, perhaps—he is apt to see three wraithlike shapes in black dragging a struggling boy with dripping hair into the icy waters of Dead Man's Pond….

Ghost Riders

Dorothy Davies

Seven of us rode into the hick town, packing guns, dead men and bad luck. We'd been a group of ten live men when we started out, friends looking for adventure, gold, action and some shooting practice, preferably a bad man or two to be put down. That's how Jack The Man saw it, always said that: 'any bad men here to be put down?'

It caused a riot when we said that in a saloon. The place usually went into uproar and we would be bombarded with drinks, often more than we could handle and, let me tell you, that took some doing.

Some called us bounty hunters but really we did it for fun. The money was a bonus. Most times people bought us drinks and stood us meals. Horses got fed and attended to, courtesy of the town once we put down the bad men. We never failed.

So there were ten of us riding into towns on fine horses with good quality harness and Spanish leather saddles. That caused some eyebrows to go up and some envy to be displayed. We'd fought hard – in a manner of speaking - for what we had, we wanted to flaunt it. Why not?

We were down to nine after the first town we hit that summer– we hit it rather hard, it seems, firing guns in all directions before heading for the drinks and the women. Someone didn't much like that, came out blasting and we were down to nine before we had a chance to look round. Todd caught it that time, full in the face as it happened: left a nasty mess.

He don't look much riding his horse these days. We have to remind ourselves that it's Todd. We wouldn't have a problem if it was just him riding like he always did, half laid back, half rigid and ever looking round for trouble - it found him, just like we always said it would - but we had the other two as well, you see; gets confusing at times. They tend to fade in and out, these ghost riders, not sure which one's which till they take a more solid form and then they go all misty again. The horses don't seem to mind one way or the other; they keep right on following us regardless.

Hardy was next, in the town right after the first one. Got himself into some fool argument over some fool woman and got shot down. Most of his head went missing somewhere. He rides a bit lopsided these days, compensating for the missing bit, I think. His ghost figure tends to fade out so far at times we think the horse is riderless, then it comes back in again and we go 'hey, Hardy's back!' and the ghost grins a death grin at us and says nothing.

Then it was Chaps. Damn fool Chaps. We miss him like you wouldn't believe. He was the life and soul of the group, him and his endless jokes that cracked us up and kept us going.

No shot there, no fool action, just keeled over and fell off his horse deader than a dried out steer. Damn fool knew he had a ticker on the way out and did nothing about it. Went right on with the

105

cigarillos and the over eating and the over acting and the over – well, you get the picture. He knew it and he wanted to go out as he lived, enjoying himself. So we were riding like always, hell for leather, he was tossing jokes at us like always, mad as hell jokes, got halfway through a cracking one and fell off. We thought he was fooling with us, made all sorts of comments 'til we realized it was for real, He weren't getting up without help.

And he was beyond help. We left the body where it fell and went on riding with the ghost.

So there we were, seven living, three dead when we were about to ride into what some called Goldrush and some called White Waters and some called End Of Line and others had names so coarse even I wouldn't say them. That's saying something, I can tell you.

Jack The Man said it was a bit of a shame Chaps had gone and joined the others, 'cos we had no joker to stir us up and keep us going.

I said Jack The Man was a joker just by being alive and why couldn't he take over being the group's clown.

He said he didn't have the gift. I agreed with him there but it was a bit of a shame. He was cut out to be a joker, so he was, but he lacked the gift of fast talking. With Jack you waited half an hour or more for the punch line to any story. He liked to talk it to death.

So there we were in what I might as well call Goldrush for all it matters to you who's listening to this tale. Seven live men, three dead men and for once, no bad men to take down. Leastways, didn't see no WANTED posters anywhere. What were we gonna do with ourselves? Get us some chow and a bed for the night, prop the ghost riders up against the stable wall to watch over the horses until dawn and ride on… or was there something more in this rather strange town?

I mean…

Tom bit too much off his cheroot and spit it into the street, only to have some tidied up oldster shouting 'hey, Mister, quit with that, would ya?" which shook Tom so much he didn't come back with a smartass comment like usual.

Charlie's horse dropped a packet and someone else scurried out with shovel and bucket and shook it at Charlie like he'd done it himself. In the name of heaven, what's with this town, I thought. They'll be wanting us to clear up after our own horses next!

"Ease up, old man," I called back to the manure collector. "Supposed to be damn good for the roses, that stuff."

"We don't grow roses around here, bandit!" he yelled back and stomped off into some wooden hut that –oddly –had roses growing over the doorway. I looked at Charlie and he looked right back at me, as blank a look as I had.

I mean; what the hell…

And - bandit?

Hank rode a tad closer. "Hey, bandit!"

I grinned at him and faked a punch. "Quit it, loser!"

Pedro heeled his horse. "First one to find the saloon gets the best looking woman!" and tore off before we could respond. We all shot after him, ghost riders and all.

In fact, it were Chaps who got there first but he weren't no good with the women any more so we dismissed that and let the honour go to Juan who beat Pedro by a nose, his horse's nose, not his. Although come to think of it, Juan's nose was pretty damn big.

So we pushed open the doors of the saloon and swaggered in, heading for the bar – which was selling milk by the look of it. And big machines that looked like they vended anything but whiskey or beer.

The girl was all right, though, pink cheeks, red lips and rather a prominent bay window, if you know what I mean. Don't ask me to spell it out.

"Welcome, gentlemen," she said, with the brightest smile this side of sundown. "All of you," she added, looking past us at the empty saddles outside. "Are your friends coming in?"

"Well, no," Hank was took by surprise and it showed. "They're dead, actually."

"Oh I know," she smiled again, bigger this time, if that be possible. "I can see they're dead, shot to bits, two of them and one dead of a heart attack, right?"

We stared at her, all seven of us in a row, all covered in trail dust, muck and – don't ask about the rest, sometimes we ain't too careful where we lays down at night – dying of thirst, needing a drink and a few bad men to take down and she's talking about our dead companions like she knew all about them.

"Yes," I said eventually, like some fumbling bumbling schoolkid with a crush on the teacher. Well, she was kinda pretty and she knew too much. Way too much.

"Well," she pulled some levers and steam rocketed out of the machines. We backed off, fast. "Ask them in."

She put cups on the counter, cups, I ask you – with coffee in them, rich dark coffee with swirls of cream floating on top. Ten cups.

I counted them and then went to the doors.

"Hey guys," I looked at them sitting there, sort of fading in and out, "the girl in here's serving coffee and told me to come and invite you all in."

They looked at one another and slid down off their horses, walked up the steps through the doors I held open and went straight to the counter. Couldn't call it a bar any more.

"Welcome to the town," she said, pushing cups at us. "So glad you arrived, we need some fresh blood here."

I saw Todd go *thank you* as best he could with half a face and she bobbed a curtsey, I swear she did. Chaps wrapped a hand around the cup and, although I never saw it leave the counter, the coffee done disappeared. I looked over and Hardy was doing the same thing. Cup on the counter, coffee gone into what should have been a ghost stomach. But it couldn't have been, cos it didn't leak all over the floor.

Which was not sawdusted but polished.

Just what sort of town had we ridden into?

The doors slammed and the Sheriff strolled in, all pressed uniform, gleaming badge and immaculate shave.

"Welcome, gentlemen," said in a rich voice that sounded like honey and whiskey combined.

"Thank you," said a mixed bunch of voices. All of us speaking at once.

"I see you have spooks with you." He nodded at the three ghost riders. "Good to see you here. Not often we get the chance to talk with those on the other side of life."

What in the name of – was he talking about?

Pedro nudged me and made the sign of the cross. "I don't like this place, compadre," he whispered.

"Neither do I," I whispered back, "but we're stuck here for a little while."

"Sure, sure. Just don't make it too long, eh?"

"I hear you."

And I did but I was intrigued and it's been a lifetime or two since I got intrigued with anything. I mean, I ride with dead men, so it takes something special to intrigue me, right?

The sheriff spun round on his highly polished heels which looked like he never stepped in a speck of dust in his life. Come to think on it, the road outside was cleaner than the last bar we hit, so perhaps he hadn't.

"The people of this town welcome those who are no longer living," he said, so pompous you would have thought he was the head honcho or something. Perhaps he was. "We rarely get the chance to meet and greet such people, so I trust you will do us the great favour of staying for a few days."

"Well, we were searching for some bad men to take down," Jack The Man said, rather hesitantly. "Like, it's a way we earn our money, see?"

"I understand that." Damn me if he didn't puff himself up a bit more. "Perhaps we could come to some arrangement whilst you're here. For a start, let me organize stabling for your horses."

He blew a whistle, I swear to God he did that and some bright young shiny faced youngsters charged into the saloon.

"Take these horses to the stables, Julio," he ordered. "Get your friends to help if you must, but go easy with the fine animals and no one; no one is to touch the harness or saddles, right?"

"Yes, sir!" Julio saluted, sort of soldier-like and raced out the door, yelling a variety of names that got mixed up in my head. I saw our horses being led away by a bunch of kids and hoped to hell I wasn't making a big mistake here. My coffee had gone cold; the pretty thing behind the counter poured me another from the big machine without my asking. I didn't dare show my ignorance and ask what it was. I didn't dare show my ignorance and ask if she'd read my mind, either. I was getting worried about the way these people knew so much.

"Come and sit down," the sheriff invited all of us with a generous sweep of his hand. "Molly, bring me a coffee, there's a sweetheart."

"Sure, Sheriff!" You know the expression 'chirped'? I never thought I'd hear it. I just did. Like a little bird.

111

We pulled some tables together, stacked stools around them and sat with coffee. I mean, coffee, it was still hard to believe we were doing that, drinking this stuff that had no kick, outside of whatever was in the coffee beans, thinking *what the hell's going on here?* None of us spoke, we shuffled around a bit, pushed the ghosts to one side and got pushed right back again. Hardy in particular weren't having none of it.

Jack looked like he'd walked into a madhouse. Charlie didn't look much better and as for the rest of us, we just looked plain puzzled.

The sheriff's coffee arrived and he stirred it with a little silver spoon. I had to blink to be sure I weren't seeing things.

"Right, gentlemen. I can see all sorts of 'what's going on here?' expressions, so let me explain."

"That would be good," Pedro pushed his cup to one side. "Start by telling us why we can't get a decent drink in this town."

"Because drink causes problems, sir. You must know that. Can I ask, would you mind?" he gestured at the three ghosts, "did these gentlemen meet their deaths through drink related incidents?"

Juan snorted at the ponderous language. "Not all three of them, no. One, old Chaps here-" he pointed at the youngest of the three, Chaps hadn't been above thirty when he keeled over, "fell off his horse with a heart seizure. Your girl over there already spotted that and commented on it."

"Of course, Molly would have seen that straight off. Right smart she is, one of the best in the town."

Best what, I wondered.

"But to resume, gentlemen, drink causes all manner of problems, smashed up saloons, smashed up people, gunfights, blood in the street, no, we don't want that in our town. So we invested in this machine which dispenses the finest coffee and you can have cake or cookies with it."

I felt sick.

"Perhaps we should ride on?" I looked round at my friends, appealing to their better nature.

They surprised me. "We should give this a try, you know. We've never done it before." Hank, being all – what? Almost coy! Did he have his eye on the delectable Molly, I wondered.

"Well, I think I want to mosey on." I started to get up and found my legs wouldn't support me. Charlie began to laugh and then sort of fell across the table, almost lifeless.

"It's the coffee!" I managed before my voice disappeared.

"So it is." The Sheriff smiled, picked up his cup and drank it all. With no ill effects. "Molly knows which ones to give to visitors and which to give to us residents, you see."

The ghosts had folded in on themselves. Chaps was a small bundle of grey wool, Todd was half faded, the other half – the right hand side actually – was almost transparent and Hardy was – not there.

"Might as well close up for the night, Molly."

"Right, Sheriff, thank you."

In what seemed like no time, the lights went out in the saloon, the big shutter was drawn down in front of the swing doors and we were left alone. Ten of us. I still counted Hardy although I didn't know if

113

he was still there. Couldn't see a damn thing in the darkness.

I heard the horses' hooves as someone rode away with them in a line. I heard each one distinctly, knew their way of striking the ground; knew that I would never see them again.

Knew I would never ride again, either.

I had no idea what sunrise would bring but somehow nothing would surprise me anymore.

I'd just joined my companions as a ghost rider but one that was going no place very soon.

It was gonna be a long night.

Memento Mori

Liam A Spinage

He likes to make us dance. Every night, he sits cross-legged on a tomb and pulls out a little flute of carved bone wrapped in... let's call it leather. He puts it to his cracked lips and begins to play. Across the cemetery, hands force their way through disturbed dark earth, yearning to be free, their nails stained by the escape from their eternal prisons. What ragged, filthy flesh remains stretches upward, dragging hide-tanned corpses into the chill night. Those of us who have been dead longer rise slower, bone-bleached, cantankerous, and rattle our way up to join this processional of the damned, bound in service to an ancient eldritch tool now in the unworthiest of hands.

He forces me to lead, on account of my former occupation at the court, he says. I stumble and shake as the grisly parade begins, shuffling around the graveyard with no purpose other than to titillate the despotic mind of an assured lunatic. The houses he makes do not last till doomsday: they are temporary resting places only. We rarely have the fortune to end the parade in the same patch of earth in which we start.

When I first tried to rebel, to rail against this shambolic reminder of life, he removed my skull as punishment. He likes to show it to people occasionally. Not that visitors to the graveyard are frequent. "Quiet as the grave." Ha! There is nothing quiet about this mockery of life: a clacking of old bones, the soft plop of sloughing, rancid flesh as it hits the soft earth and, above all, the manic laughter of the gravedigger himself.

The dead hunger not for blood or revenge, but for rest. We are all prisoners of that unquiet mind, void of meaning. I had a tongue in me and could sing once. I was thought of as a fellow of infinite jest. Now there are no flashes of merriment left.

Alas.

The Giving Spirit

Rickey Rivers Jr.

Gilda spent the morning shopping: She wanted enough candy to strip off the label. The other parents didn't want her around. They were the ones who gave her the label. They had called her "The Widow Creep."

Gilda decided that Halloween was the perfect time to show how friendly and welcoming she actually was. She had grown sick of the label, and tired of children being afraid. She liked children, aging made her realize that. Conversations between her and others often went to sad places. She didn't wish to take them there. She never wished to upset anyone. Despite intentions, the stigma stuck. The names led to eggs being thrown and her mailbox dented. It felt strange to be bullied again. High school was so long ago.

This year she decided to change things. The candy was ready. Decorations were set. Her whole house was made to be a celebration of Halloween: translucent ghosts, black cats, orange and black streamers, skeletons and spider webs (only some were store bought, it was creepier keeping the real ones up).

She was ready for an especially spooky Halloween. Most of all she looked forward to seeing the children in their ghastly and creative costumes. Some of them were cute. Her favorites were the weird combinations. One year she saw a girl dressed as a vampire ballerina. Another year, she saw a boy dressed as a creepy snowman with a lab coat. She regretted not asking why the lab coat was essential to the costume. She came up with a scenario: a mad scientist was turned into a snowman. Then, for some reason, he became a serial killer. That made sense to her.

Coming up with little stories for the costumes was fun. One thing she could say about the neighborhood children is that they were creative. She appreciated the efforts of anyone actually trying on Halloween, considering so many adults had become cynical about the holiday.

This year she dressed up as well. It didn't take much effort. For this Halloween she became a witch, with an old black dress and a dollar store witch hat. She practiced her witchy voice in the mirror and gave up once she started to sound funny rather than scary. She couldn't manage scary when she tried.

She called herself foolish. No one was in the house to say otherwise. Several times she had thought about moving, but couldn't bring herself to leave. On occasion the loneliness would set in as a cloud. What made matters worse was her son refusing to visit. He spent most of his time with his own family, something she understood. At the same time she wanted company, she craved it. She had sought friendship with neighbors, but they never held a conversation. They always had somewhere else to go, people to see.

She was called long winded, but not to her face. She felt that many pitied her and that feeling was like guilt. Some were rude, but Gilda smiled regardless, a half-hearted crinkle. To be a good neighbor was something she wanted, something she needed. She felt it would help make her whole again. Tonight was her night, a night to prove a worth she thought she lost.

Gilda mixed candy into a big pumpkin shaped bucket: sour gum, sticky sticks, sugar bunnies, lumpy mellows and chocolate earwax. The last one was popular with the kids. The name was given to gross them out, but it instead intrigued, that and the commercials of children sticking their fingers into each other's ears. Gilda liked chocolate, but had never tried chocolate earwax. The name was a turnoff.

***

Gilda switched on the porch light and sat in the living room. She felt anxiety, catching herself looking at the wall clock every few seconds. It was still light out, there was still time. She took a moment to remember if she had taken her medicine or not. She settled on yes, but was pretty unsure.

Her mind wandered. *Would anyone actually visit?* Then the doorbell rang. The sound focused her. She grabbed the bucket of candy off the nearby coffee table and headed toward the front door. She got herself into character and opened the door with a witch-like voice.

"Well, hello children-" she stopped herself. No one was there.

She walked out onto the porch. Crunchy leaves and the whistling wind greeted her. She heard laughing somewhere, somewhere close. Children were playing ding dong ditch. That game was so old it made her remember her age. She stepped inside and shut the door. She was annoyed. The unoriginality was soul crushing.

What's next? She thought. *Toilet papering the house, eggs again?* She reminisced on childhood pranks she used to play with her friends. The thought of lighting a bag, and the contents being stomped out made her laugh.

The doorbell rang.

She got herself ready and swung open the door.

"Good evening children," she said in a witchy way.

A child stood on her porch dressed as a mummy holding an old bag for candy.

"Were you the one ringing my doorbell?"

The mummy kid shook its head.

"Oh yeah and what if I don't believe you?" She stuck her hand into the candy bucket. *"Well, you only get one candy unless you tell me."*

The mummy kid shrugged.

"Fine, here's your one single piece of candy."

She gave the mummy one piece of a candy then started to feel bad. The kid might have been innocent and shy, probably had no idea of what she was talking about. She offered him more candy in witch-like fashion.

"Okay kid, since you're the first one I'll give you a few more, but only because I like your costume."

She gave the mummy a handful of candy.

"Now go, bring a crowd next time."

The mummy kid didn't move.

"Don't be greedy or I'll send you back to your tomb."

The mummy kid lowered the candy bag and turned away.

She felt bad.

"Hey, wait!" she called, much too loud for earshot

The mummy kid turned to face her.

"Uh, when did mummies come back in style?"

This kid can't leave with a bad impression of me, she thought.

"Haven't seen a mummy in a long time, back in the day my folks use to watch the black and white movies. Maybe your parents remember them?"

The mummy shook its head in a way that seemed sad. *Oh no!* She thought. *Maybe he doesn't have parents, or they're not around?* She tried to keep conversation light.

"Or just look up the old stuff?" Gears were shifted. "Anyway, seeing a real mummy is a treat. I used to dress up like a witch back in the day. I mean, before I became one."

She laughed, felt awkward about it and smiled. At this point she completely forgot about the witch voice.

"You know, Ronnie hated Halloween for some reason. He didn't even wanna pass out candy." She paused. "Would you like to hear about him, my Ronnie?"

The mummy nodded.

"He was a military man, a real serious type. All of them aren't like that, but he was that way until he got a few drinks in him. Then again, I guess everyone gets that way if they get drunk." She laughed, thought about it, and redirected.

"Anyway, we met at a nightclub years ago. I was sitting by myself and this tall, dark haired handsome man walked up to me. Maybe it'll sound cheesy now, but he held out his hand and asked me directly if I'd like to dance. Now I was young so to me there was something romantic about being asked so direct, by a military man no less! Kid, he had on the uniform and everything!

"Before I knew it I was swept off my feet. We danced all night, it was fun. We didn't keep much contact after that, he went to the war. When he came back, a short while later we were married. The wedding was just...beautiful, white and gold. I actually got to know more about him after the marriage. I guess we kind of rushed into it, but it's easy to say that now. At the time, it felt right, you know?"

The mummy kid nodded.

"He was a good man." She went on. "Knew how to dress and treated me right, better than any other man I ever met. They'll never be another man like him. Not for me. Not like I tried looking either. No reason to..."

Her eyes watered.

122

"Hey, I'm sorry kid. You don't need to see me like this. I'm getting choked up."

She wasn't prepared for how hard the memories hit her. She felt a shiver, wrapped her arms around herself. The Halloween night blew directly into her home. It passed her without care. Her voice weakened.

"Here's some more candy, kid." She gave the mummy another handful.

"Thanks for listening. I know I talk a lot, but I've got no one else to talk to. And hey, for a mummy you're a great listener."

The mummy kid nodded.

"Great work on the costume too. Is it homemade?"

The mummy kid nodded.

"Come on kid, you can talk to me."

With that, the mummy kid dropped the bag of candy on the porch, the bandages unwrapped and followed suit. Within an instant the wind blew and carried the bandages off into the night. It happened so fast that Gilda could barely comprehend it. On impulse she responded with anger.

"You're welcome, I guess!"

She gathered the bag of fallen candy and promptly slammed the front door.

"Kid didn't even take the candy and had the nerve to not even exist!"

She threw the mummy's candy bag on the living room couch and tossed her bucket of candy into the kitchen.

"Just my luck, I knew a mummy was out of place. You can't trust a mummy costume. Kids don't even know about mummies!"

Gilda paced back and forth. She felt taken advantage of, it was irrational, but so was the situation. In her mind being irrational made the most sense in the world.

"Whatever!" she said to no one.

She stopped pacing and plopped down on the couch, crushing the candy bag beneath her.

"I don't care!"

She tried her best to hold back the tears but couldn't. She put her head in her hands and broke down, "stupid mummy."

A rustling within the house quieted her. Someone was there. She stood up from the couch. Her eyes went upstairs with her mind.

How did something get in?

There was a creak on the top step of the staircase, a footstep. Then there was another. Gilda went to the kitchen, nearly slipping on the spilled candy inside and grabbed a knife from the knife holder. There was another step, then another, and Gilda waited in the kitchen with the kitchen knife.

Her breathing slowed. Her eyes were focused. Her heart was racing. She thought about Ronnie and wished he was there to protect her. Then with another step she saw the military uniform, the same one from the closet, the same one Ronnie wore so long ago.

Gilda dropped the kitchen knife. It made a sound that didn't matter and she approached the impossible person who approached her.

"Can't be you," she said, taking a step from the kitchen to the living room. "It can't be you."

The military man stood tall in the living room with one hand outstretched. In the living room light the outstretched hand seemed barely there. Gilded placed a hand in his.

"Ronnie," she said.

He pulled her close and said no words. Her mind went to dancing and her body followed. The military man moved with her slow, this way, that, her hand in his, one hand on her back, her hand on his shoulder. They danced this way for some time. She put her head on his chest.

"Ronnie," she said. "I miss you so much."

The military man said nothing and danced. All the while Gilda heard music surround her. It was the same song she had heard before, their song. Every memory hit her at once, the proposal, the Beach vacation, Ronnie's return from the war, the birth of Grayson, the many times they forgot each other's medicine, every laugh they shared. Each moment was a picture in her head, a continuous illumination. Nothing was a moment of fear, of anger, of sadness, everything given in the now was happiness.

Gilda wept dancing. It felt like she was dancing in every room. It felt like she had no body, only the military man to carry her anywhere he pleased. After a time, the weight of her partner became less and less. And the military man dissipated.

She was on the steps now in a daze. She was smiling. Gilda moved through the living room light as a feather, light as she was on the night of her proposal. Her heart felt like it could float above the trees and disappear into a cloud.

All at once the weight of the world came down on her and she stumbled as she drifted from room to room. She took a moment and rested. Then she smiled to herself. Her head was spinning. The night overwhelmed her, this night, and every other night she saw.

She gathered herself and went to the kitchen. Candy was sprawled all over the floor along with the kitchen knife. Some of the candies were crushed. She searched for a particular one and smiled when she saw it.

Slowly she leaned and grabbed a piece of chocolate earwax. She peeled the wrapper, smelled it and put the candy into her mouth. Gilda walked back through the living room, smiling at a picture of Ronnie. Then she winced, the candy was terrible.

This night was a special night. On this night every neighbor in this particular neighborhood was visited by a particular trick or treater. They all had a story to share, but they all seemed to like Gilda's most of all. Especially the children, they loved when she used her witchy voice.

Tell No Tales

Liam A Spinage

Gather round, gather round. I'm here to tell a story. You've probably heard parts of it before. Throughout the length and breadth of the bay, this story has been told anew with each rising tide. Every time it varies a little. Small changes are made, embellishments emphasizing local character by those who were at the telling of it, or by those who were at the telling of a telling of it and so on as each tale trickles down like a little stream finding its way to the shore. And each of them does find its own way, though they flow eventually into that self-same sea where these events first happened.

The story goes something like this. I swear by my own experiences of the past three weeks that it's all true, so help me God.

Somewhere in the bay is a hidden island lost in banks of mist and surrounded by dangerous shoals. On that island is a vast amount of buried treasure. Every pirate captain in their day once berthed on its only safe beach, accompanied by the newest members of their crew, oblivious to what was about to happen. These unknowing sailors carried a chest of ill-gotten gains to a lonely cave or a hidden cove or a turn in the river, where there lies a deep pit at the base of an old, gnarled tree. When they laid the last of the treasure in that pit, a face appeared in the bark, green eyes glowing with malevolent energy.

127

Branches reached down and grabbed them, hurling them into the sacrificial pit where quick-running sands and fast-flowing waters seeped over them and buried them alive. Then the tree screamed like the gull in the storm, a cry that mingled with the wind in the dead wood of its branches or the waves shrilling on the outer beach. Even the cruelest of buccaneers shivered as they heard that wail. Yet each captain knew that their treasure was safe, its whereabouts protected by an ancient evil, paid for with lost souls and the silence of the grave.

Spooky, huh? I was perfectly placed to recall the tales that were told in tavern and villa alike and how could I not be? I have been writing and performing variations on the tale since I first heard it. I had sought out every account I could find and confabulated them into stirring scripts of comedy, tragedy, morality and horror alike. That summer our performances were praised in every parlor, toasted in every tavern. No one had a greater collection of these stories than I. We sailed in the wake of these tales and for a while were the singular sensation of the summer. After several years languishing at the bottom of every playbill, it seemed we had finally found our fortune. Even when innumerable encores tested us to the point of exhaustion, we managed to shine throughout the night as bright as the stars themselves. I never considered for one moment that there was truth in those tales. Until a certain map came into my possession: the result of a sotted quartermaster and a lost wager.

The seasonal performances had ended at that point and had left us with a reasonable sum which we could have invested in a new play or idled away in luxury until the day our indolence exceeded our funds. But we wanted more. And I had in my possession the key not only to this great treasure, but the story that came with it. A story we could live. if only we were bold enough. A story I could retell. This story.

We spent three days arguing about what to do and a matter of hours finding a captain with equal measures of greed and foolhardiness who might see our dreams fulfilled. We tramped the gangplank of The Hasty Maiden without a care in the world, our heads swimming with the tang of salt and adventure.

Now, Captain Juanita Argentina was a harsh woman with a harsh crew, but cheap, willing and available. Too willing, perhaps. That should have been our first clue. We had been uncomfortable about showing her the map until we were underway, but now we unfolded it in her cabin and all looked at it intently.

"Three days sail south along the coast, two tacking to the southwest and a further day on the open waves. That should do it. We'll make landfall in no time: the winds will favor us outward bound but the return voyage will be trickier." She looked up. "Any of you ever sailed before?" She did not look surprised when we all replied in the negative, merely dismissed us with a wave of her tattooed hand and strode out on the deck to shout orders to her band of miscreants and misfits.

I'll spare you the details of the journey. I can see you're all familiar with such things. Suffice to say that we enjoyed the trip immensely, got in the way of operations and generally made a nuisance of ourselves. For the most part, I was fascinated by ship life and dedicated myself to learning everything I could of my new environment as fodder for future fantasies. The sea behaved, the winds were with us and nothing unfortunate occurred. I can tell from your mumblings that you think that in itself is unusual. But what were we to know? We were actors, not sailors. Our waves were ribbons of blue and white, our boat an upturned table. Despite initial appearances, the captain ran a tight ship and we arrived at the island on the day appointed and not a moment before or after. That, of course, is where the adventure began in earnest.

Once we had navigated the eerie fog which surrounded the place and narrowly avoided the shoals only by virtue of them being marked on our map, the captain called for us. We were to join her and her alone in a rowing boat and make our way to the place marked. The crew would remain to take care of the ship and make repairs to the rigging in readiness for our return. She bade us carry a small chest down to the boat. Since she didn't tell us not to look inside, we did. There were three small shovels, an axe, a good length of rope and a barrel of gunpowder. When we asked, she grinned. "That damned tree will never see what's coming." She spoke this with a degree of smug satisfaction that it mollified any reticence we had. That was our second warning. It's difficult, you see, even when you know the story, to see it when you're living it. It's like what they say inland about wood and trees.

There was a slow rise at the edge of the shore and we picked our way toward it over the hot sand. The sun beat down on our backs as the beach became spotted with clumps of grass and reeds. Small pools of brackish water spotted the marshland just over that rise, shrouded in a low hanging mist which clung to us with clammy hands as we tried to get bearings from our map of the island. There were few trees here at all and none of them seemed to be in the right place. This did not slow the captain's pace one jot. Whenever she turned back to admonish us for moving too slowly, what little of her face we could see between hat and throat seemed locked in a foreboding grimace which did nothing to raise our cheer or allay our fears.

We spent a full three hours crossing that marsh, leeches on our legs and flies on our face. By the time we reached a low hillock of dry ground, we were exhausted. And there, lonely as a lost soul, was the dead tree shown on the old quartermaster's map. What sighs of relief we made! The end of an arduous trek, the promise of wealth, the malodorous fumes of the marsh, they each made us giddy in different ways.

"Here it is. Get those shovels out and show us what you're made of!" None of us noticed the captain's voice dropping a register. None of us hesitated to start digging. We were full of the wonder of the moment, resurgent after all the energy spent trudging through saltmarsh. We didn't even notice when her eyes flashed green for a moment. A trick of the light, perhaps. We were used to those on the stage. The first thing we noticed was when the branches of the tree began to move a moment later, creaking into a facsimile of life. Rotted roots reached for our ankles even as thick, knobbled branches began to lash out at our arms and faces.

The captain was laughing full-throated now, a raucous racket which came from somewhere beyond this earth, her head bent back in gloating triumph. Three more bodies for the pit. Three more unwary souls for her infernal bargain.

That's when I rushed forward unsuspectingly, barreled into her and knocked her backward into the waterlogged pit. She hung mid-air for a moment and with wide-eyed horror saw the moment of her undoing. Pale figures gathered above her around the pit mouth: ghosts of those who had been killed here, sacrificed to this ancient effigy of wickedness beneath whose roots lay wealth unimaginable. As she opened her mouth to plead for mercy, a pale figure rose from the depths and wrapped its cold fingers around her neck. More followed, spectral clammy hands grasping at her but ignoring us. As the captain gasped for breath, the pit collapsed around her, burying her in a watery grave. The tree fell silent.

We rested there awhile until we realized we should get back and signal the ship, to try and explain what had happened to the captain. When we reached the beach, however, there was no sign of it. We slept under the stars and vowed to tackle our mounting problems in the morning.

Now, I hate to be a spoilsport but here is the lay of things. We spent three days on that island doing

132

nothing but digging with those shovels and drinking our fill of coconut water. At the end of that time, we still hadn't found any sign of buried treasure. Not a pearl or a sapphire or a single piece of eight. I tell you now, there's no reward to be had there. Danger, sure. A curse, absolutely. But no treasure. When we were rescued on the fourth day by a passing merchantman, we disembarked at the first port and vowed never to take to sea again or speak of what had happened.

It might seem strange, then, that I'm telling you this now. Truth is, we sunk all our funds in that venture and it came to nothing. I only ask that you reach into your pockets for a modest amount of coin, to ease the aching in this storyteller's throat and afford me a few minor comforts. I thank you.

***

It was a little later, as I stood alone on the dock, that I was approached by an elderly seafaring gentleman who had been in the crowd earlier.

"That's a fine story. It's a shame about the treasure. Just a story, right?"

I nodded. He seemed to want to say more.

"It's just that I couldn't help noticing that doubloon you paid for your meal with. Reckon as that's an old, old, coin. One that might come from an old, old, story."

I turned to him and winked. We smiled at each other in the dead of night, the only noise the gentle lapping of waves.

Then I stared at him, long and hard and deep, my eyes suddenly glowing a hideous shade of green, my voice a harsh screech heard throughout the years. I shrieked loud and long like a gull across the bay, louder than the ocean itself.

The Day Punk Rock Saved the World

Jason R Frei

Razzle stomped down the sidewalk. The thick soles of his Doc Marten's clomped an angry beat, matching the scowl on his face. He hated Halloween—all the wannabes, the posers, the imposters. He hated their fake, syrupy blood and their rubbery masks and their cheap commercial-bought, flimsy costumes. He wanted to knock them over, stomp on them and set the world on fire.

He especially hated all the fakers on South Street who dressed up as punk rockers. They all wore the same thing—black leather pants, the obligatory punk rock t-shirt (either Ramones or Sex Pistols) under a new pleather jacket and cheap plastic boots. They all sneered like Billy Idol, knowing nothing of his life in Generation X. They were spoon-fed heaping crapfuls of new wave imitation punk from MTV and Hot Topic. They didn't know the roots of 1960's and 1970's punk, or the 1980's hardcore, Oi! and anarcho-punk scene.

Razzle took pride in his beat-up leather biker jacket with a hand painted white Crass symbol on the back. Hand-punched and threaded metal spikes adorned the bottoms of the sleeves. Pins featuring the Dead Kennedys, Black Flag, Conflict and Rudimentary Peni studded the front lapels. Underneath his jacket was a torn, black Subhumans t-shirt. A red and black plaid shirt, tied around his waist, hung down in the back over ripped black jeans.

What made him truly stand out from the posers was his eight-inch tall Liberty Spike mohawk. The brown-almost-black, blond-tipped hair stood straight up, stiff with Knox gelatin. His hair was his pride and joy. He woke up two hours early every morning to get each spike perfectly straight.

It wasn't just the way he dressed that made him punk. Punk was an attitude, a way of life, a community. If you were part of the culture, you were family. The people who played pretend and dressed up like them shit all over his family.

Razzle seethed at the disrespect and, at first, didn't notice the dirty bum dressed as Elvis approaching him from the street. The man looked drunk, lurching to and fro. Razzle turned the dial up on his Walkman as GBH blared out about a city baby being attacked by rats, hoping it would drown out any plea for spare change.

The man's lips moved in a mumbled way and Razzle noticed the decay and filth on the man's teeth and ashen face.

"Get away, fucker," he yelled. "I ain't got no money on me."

The man continued stumbling toward him, hands reaching out. The punk side-stepped the bum and pushed him hard back into the street. He laughed and threw a middle finger over his shoulder. Moments later, he felt a hand grab one of his Liberty spikes. Razzle reached into his jacket pocket and slid his fingers into a set of brass

136

knuckles. He turned quickly, clenched his fist and punched the grimy Elvis-impersonator in the face. The man fell to the ground. Razzle stomped on his head with his big black boots. Blood and fluid sprayed the sidewalk.

He kicked the vagrant one more time in the ribs.

"Never touch my fucking hair!"

He put the knucks back in his pocket and turned to the window in the nearest shop, relieved that his hair was still in line. He turned, spat on the downed man and stalked off.

***

The atmosphere inside Zipperhead was like a lit powder keg ready to blow. Holly Hell stood at the glass counter, trying her hardest not to punch the couple she was talking to.

"I told you," she said through clenched teeth. "There's no discount and we don't take checks. Cash or credit only."

A mid-thirties man wearing chinos and a Moby t-shirt argued with her. "Four hundred bucks for a used leather jacket? C'mon lady. Nobody'll buy that!"

"It's vintage and I should charge you more for the way you're dressed. Now, either cash, credit or get the fuck out!"

Razzle slinked in and quietly stood behind the couple.

The woman customer had a bored air about her. She held one arm across her brown and tan button-

137

down shirt and her other arm angled off to the side like she was waiting for a tip. The shirt draped untucked over faded-blue drainpipe jeans that ended in a pair of patent leather winklepickers. Heavy purple eye shadow darkened lids that were half closed. A multi-colored Caesar cut framed her pale face. She channeled a Southern and slurred Marilyn Monroe when she spoke.

"Darling," she drawled. "Just put it on the card."

Razzle doubled over from laughter. The whole scene was bizarre, like something from a David Lynch movie. The man turned around.

"What are you laughing at, dickhead?"

The laughter died in Razzle's throat. His face turned red and his nostrils flared. He raised his fists for a fight. Holly Hell rapped gently on the counter. When the couple turned back toward her, she pointed a nail-studded bat at them.

"Both of you. Out. Now!" The words came out as a deep growl and the veins popped out on her neck.

The bored lady huffed, as if violence meant nothing to her. She pulled a roll of money from inside her shirt.

"I'll give you six hundred. Cash."

When the sale was completed and the couple walked out, Razzle laughed, reached over the counter and tousled Holly Hell's platinum blond hair.

"Where'd you get that archaic device?"

138

She hefted the bat. "Chango brought it in the other day. Said a couple shops down the street got robbed and didn't want me here defenseless."

"How sweet of him." Razzle looked around the shop. "Allison been by yet?"

"Not yet. You two got a date?"

"Dead Milkmen at the Troc tonight. Halloween tradition. And we're just friends."

Right on cue, a Spanish girl in a tight Exploited tank top, checkered wool skirt and fishnets walked in. Her hair was buzzed short, black with orange spots. Razzle knew her back when she was still Alan. Then she got kicked out of her house and had nowhere to go. The Philly punk scene took her in and became her family. They helped transform her into the fiery, mocha-skinned Puerto Rican with a tucked penis and a padded bra that she was today.

,She greeted Razzle and Holly Hell in her normal vulgar manner. "Hey fuckers."

Holly Hell grinned. "Slut."

"You know it."

Razzle opened his mouth for a quick retort when an older woman in a fur coat ran into the store, crying and screaming. Two gouges ruined her face and blood dripped down the front of her coat. She collapsed on the floor and went still.

People ran past the store, screaming. Razzle stepped outside and saw the Elvis-impersonator hunched over a young man, chewing on his neck. Blood spurted between his foul teeth and ran down his chin. A woman dressed as Cleopatra, missing half an arm and covered in blood, grabbed a skinhead in a muscle shirt and sank her teeth into his bicep. She wrenched her head back and pulled the muscle clean off his arm.

Razzle surveyed the street and witnessed other grisly sights. A mailman with half a face gnawed on a cop. A child, maybe seven or eight years old, pulled out her mother's entrails and slurped them into her mouth like spaghetti. Two prostitutes fought over the headless corpse of a john. Razzle slid back in the store and clicked the security lock. The girls looked at him.

"It's day of the living dead out there."

They rushed to the front window. Carnage and mayhem ruled the street out front. Fires raged in several store fronts. Cars smashed into light poles. Undead chased the living and devoured them.

"What are we gonna do?" asked Allison.

Razzle pulled down a display rack and yanked out a thick, solid metal rod. Punk t-shirts spilled over the floor. He grinned. "We arm ourselves."

He turned back to another display when a piercing shriek split the air. He turned as the old lady in the fur coat sat up and reached her clawing hands for Allison's leg.

"Hit her!" yelled Razzle.

Holly Hell stood, dumb-founded. "With what?"

"The bat in your hand, dumbass!"

She started, realizing she still held the bat. She swung down hard and connected with the reaching hand. Bones crunched and black blood splattered across the red-and-white checkered floor.

"In the head! Hit her in the head!"

The undead woman gnashed her teeth and grunted while crawling slowly across the floor. The counter girl stared in disgust at the old woman. Allison grabbed the bat out of her hand and swung. The bat hit solidly and the woman's head burst, spraying bone, blood and brain matter across the front glass counter. The body dropped to the floor and laid still.

Silence pervaded the shop until a pounding started on the front door. Both girls let out a strangled shriek and Razzle jumped. Holly Hell turned to the door and saw Chango banging. She ran over, unlocked the dead bolt and pulled the door open.

Razzle opened his mouth to yell, but it was too late. The undead Chango stumbled through the door and grabbed Holly Hell by the shoulders. He bent in as if going for a kiss and then bit into her face. Panicked and in pain, she yanked her head back. The zombie's teeth remained clamped on the skin of her cheek and her flesh flayed off like the peel off a banana.

Chango shoved the girl to the floor and lurched toward Allison. She swung with the bat, but the zombified shop owner threw an arm up and deflected the blow. The nails in the bat bit down into the flesh and stuck fast. He jerked his arm to the side and disarmed Allison in one motion.

The creature's eyes showed no emotion as it advanced. They were the color of dead steel. His teeth snapped open and shut. He reached for the Puerto Rican girl again when his head jerked violently to the side. A loud, muted thump sounded from the pipe in Razzle's hands as it smacked twice into the zombie's head. The beast turned slowly.

Razzle twisted back and exploded into motion. The pipe hit squarely into Chango's forehead, embedding his jet black devilock into the enormous dent in his head. The gray light in the creature's eyes dulled as it toppled over, finally at rest.

Holly Hell lay on the floor, looking more and more like her name every minute. Both Razzle and Allison knew the basic rules about zombies. First, they were mindless creatures bent only on eating living human flesh and organs. They saw this first hand. Second, they were not as fast as normal humans. This rule seemed to bend a little as Chango came through the door pretty fast, but that could also have been perception laced with adrenaline. The third and final rule was that anyone bitten by a zombie would also turn into a zombie. Books, movies, scientific journals and opinions all differed on how quickly this could take, but it was a certainty nonetheless.

The two punks looked down at their friend, seemingly dead on the floor. They watched for any sign that she would spring back up and try to eat them.

"What do we do?" asked Allison.

"I guess it depends."

"On what?"

"Well, we can leave her here and lock the door on the way out. That way, she's trapped in the place she loved the most."

Allison raised her eyebrows. "Or?"

"Or we can bash her head in and spare her the indignity of becoming a zombie."

Allison reached down and pulled the spiked bat from the now-truly-dead Chango. She turned and raised the bat over her head, poised for the killing blow. The bat hovered in the air for what seemed a lifetime, trembling slightly from the hands that held it. A tear trickled slowly down Allison's cheek. Her arms began to droop as her resolve faltered.

Without any warning, Holly Hell sat up and let out a long, raspy groan. Allison yelped and brought the bat down again and again until nothing was left but a gelatinous, pulpy mess of black sludge. Razzle grabbed her arms. She dropped the bat and collapsed into his embrace.

***

Allison sat on the stairs to the second floor. Her eyes were vacant. From time to time, her small body shook uncontrollably.

Razzle re-locked the door and propped several clothing racks in front. He found a large blanket with the blood-spattered face of GG Allin peering from it. He used it to cover the lone shop window. From time to time, he shifted the shirts and glanced through the front door. It seemed like the initial chaos was over, but more undead than living shuffled along the sidewalks and streets.

He looked over his shoulder at Allison. "We'll have to move out soon to get food and supplies. I don't want to get stuck out there at night."

She continued to sit and stare, her eyes wide and glazed. Razzle walked over and put a hand on her shoulder and spoke to her gently. "Ally. We've

143

been through a lot in the past few hours and I know it's hard. This... catastrophe can't be much worse than the shit you went through at home. You're a survivor and you're the toughest person I know. We can do this, together."

She looked up at him with her big, brown eyes and he saw the sanity returning little by little. He smiled and nodded his head. She nodded back.

She stood up and slapped the smooth part of the bat into the palm of her hand. "Let's go."

***

They slipped out through a security door in the back storeroom. The alleyway was shaded from the sun. Smoke drifted by lazily like small storm clouds. Razzle and Allison crept slowly, their ears and eyes open for any sign of trouble.

They were inching carefully past a large green dumpster when a padlock on a chain shot out from the darkness and hit Razzle in the knee. He cried out in pain and dropped to the ground. Allison immediately stepped over his body and raised her bat, ready to take on a horde of zombies if she had to

The bored Marilyn Monroe from earlier in the day stepped out from behind the dumpster, a length of chain running from her leather-gloved hands.

She dropped the chain and ran into Allison's arms, crying hysterically. "Oh my God! I'm so sorry. I thought you were one of them."

Razzle groaned and sat up, holding on to his knee.

144

"What the fuck, lady—wait, you!"

He recognized her instantly. She was wearing the leather jacket that caused the argument with Holly Hell. His anger flared when he realized that this woman was a cause of distress shortly before his friend's death.

"Where's your douchebag boyfriend?"

Reality slapped the woman across her face. "He's dead and he wasn't my boyfriend."

Allison squeezed her arm. "I'm sorry."

"Don't be. That worthless piece of shit was my pimp."

"What happened?" asked Razzle. His voice was softer, less of an edge to it.

"After we left the shop, some skinhead freak attacked us. Donnie, my pimp"—she glared at Razzle—"got bit and he turned into one of them. He attacked me, but luckily, his teeth couldn't bite through this jacket. I pushed him back and he smacked his head real hard on the dumpster. You'll have to thank your friend for selling me this jacket."

Allison winced, but said nothing. She glanced at Razzle and waited for him to talk.

"We're trying to get to a store that will have supplies so we can wait this out. I think there's a bodega down the corner if you'd like to follow along."

"Thank you. I'm Nat, by the way." Razzle and Allison introduced themselves as they traveled through the alleyway. They paused at the end. Smoke and screams billowed past. Shadows of fire danced on the smoke and sound was distorted, muted.

145

A white panel van drove past the alleyway. A large smiling cow with crossed-out eyes was painted on the side. On top of the van was a thin man with long, black hair yelling through a bullhorn.

"The Trocadero is safe, people. All living are welcome. We have food, water and enough music to party right through the zombie apocalypse."

A crowd of zombies shuffled after the van. Every time the man stopped shouting, he reached into a crate, pulled out an empty bottle and threw it at a zombie.

Razzle clamped his hand over his mouth, giggling hysterically. The girls looked at him as if he'd lost his mind.

He wiped a tear from his cheek. "That was Rodney Anonymous and I'm pretty sure Dean Clean was driving. The fucking Dead Milkmen are fighting off the hordes of zombies by themselves."

Nat and Allison broke into laughter and Razzle let out a war whoop. All three rushed around the corner onto South Street and ran down to the corner bodega. They spotted an open window up on the second floor and helped each other up the fire escape.

They found themselves inside a darkened apartment. It looked abandoned, but they all knew looks could be deceiving. Weapons raised, they moved silently through the rooms and then into the hall.

Razzle led the way with his iron rod. They located the door to the shop, but it was locked. Nat smiled and motioned for the other two to move away and keep an eye out. She pulled a bobby pin out of her hair and went to work on the lock. Less than ten seconds later, it clicked and the door opened. The trio set to work gathering as much food, water and emergency supplies they could find. A small rack of sporting equipment held both duffle bags and backpacks that they filled to overflowing.

Razzle set the filled bags by the open door. He turned to gather more bags when a body fell out of the ceiling tiles and landed on his back. He scuttled backwards as a young girl in a dirty blue dress stood up and advanced on him. She couldn't have been more than ten years old and looked like one of the twins from *The Shining*. Her left arm and leg were bent at impossible angles, most likely due to the fall. Her teeth clicked as she limped toward him. Razzle's iron rod lay by the door where it fell when she dropped on top of him.

He continued dragging himself backward when his pant leg snagged on the end cap of a display. He pulled and twisted, but went nowhere. The little girl lunged on top of him and bit down hard. The girl's teeth shattered. Around Razzle's neck was a dog choker chain that he wore as a necklace. A Master padlock connected the two ends of the chain. The girl had bitten down on this.

He reached out and grabbed anything he could off the shelf to keep the girl away from him. His hand landed on a package of wooden bamboo skewers. He thrust the entire pack bottom first into the girl's face. The skewers pierced the bag and went right through the creature's eyes and into its brain. The little girl slumped over onto Razzle's chest as if she were sleeping. He rolled her off and unfastened his pant leg from the display.

The fight for his life lasted mere seconds, but felt like a lifetime. Allison and Nat rushed around the corner toward him. They stopped in their tracks when they heard footsteps thumping down the stairs.

"Get the bags and close the door," said Razzle.

Allison frantically pulled the bags from the opening. Allison slammed the door shut, but it didn't close all the way. Four split and cracked fingers groped through the crack in the door. Razzle ran up with a set of kitchen shears from aisle seven. He lopped off the fingers one by one. Black goo dripped down the frame of the door, but it finally shut. Nat twisted the lock closed and meaty fists hammered at the door from the other side.

The girls looked at the shears in Razzle's hand. "My elementary school report card always said, 'Runs with Scissors'".

The joke broke the tension and they laughed.

"What now?" asked Allison.

Razzle shrugged. "I think our only hope of survival right now is to get to the Troc. You heard Rodney. There's other people holed up there and we can stay that way for a while."

Allison nodded, but Nat looked unsure.

"How are we supposed to get there?"

"Can either of you hotwire a car?"

Both girls shook their heads.

"Well, unless we can find a car with the keys in it, we'll have to walk. It's about a mile and a half, so

148

I figure, going nice and slow, it should take us about an hour."

Nat forced out a slow breath. "An hour is a long time in the middle of the zombie apocalypse."

Allison agreed. "Especially in the dark."

The trio looked outside. The sun was a blood red sliver barely visible over Jim's Steaks across the street.

Razzle picked up three of the bags and slung his pipe over his shoulder. "I guess we better get started then."

***

The punks zig-zagged through alleys, slunk behind burned-out cars and ducked into vandalized storefronts as they made their way toward the Trocadero. Old Saint Joseph's Catholic Church, the intersection of Fourth and Walnut, was jam packed with crashed cars and slowly shuffling zombies. Razzle scouted ahead a few dozen feet at a time and then hand-signaled the girls to follow.

They were almost through the intersection when the top half of a black man dressed in a purple 1970's zoot suit crawled out from under a car and grabbed Allison's legs. He yanked her down to the street and clambered over her body. Nat didn't have a clear shot with her chain and was afraid to yell out to Razzle.

The zombie bit down on Allison's breast and tore into her, knocking her head hard off the concrete. Nat hauled the half-man off of Allison by

149

its entrails-dripping waist. She slammed him down onto a manhole cover, shattering his skull.

By this time, Razzle observed the end of the fight and ran back to them. When he got to Allison, he saw the tattered shirt. He dropped to his knees next to her and sobbed. He was tired and angry for all of the friends he lost this day. He felt defeated and was ready to sit there and have it end.

Nat reached down and squeezed his shoulder. At the same time, Allison groaned and moved. Razzle picked up his pipe and raised it for the killing blow. Allison opened her brown eyes and looked at him. He saw the pain and fear in those eyes and he lowered his weapon.

"Ally?"

She sat up and looked down at her shirt. Part of the skull and Mohawk of the Pushead logo was torn out. She laughed and pulled out her ruined bra. The cup and most of the padding were destroyed, but her chest underneath was smooth and unmarred.

"Thank God I never got breasts implanted."

Razzle laughed and wrapped her in his arms. They held each other tight for as long as they could, until Nat interrupted.

"Guys. I'm all for happy occasions, but we're still balls deep in a crowd of zombies.

The punks pulled away and wiped tears from each other's eyes. Razzle helped Allison up and placed his most treasured item—his leather jacket—around her shoulders.

"This should keep you from getting bit again."

Miraculously, their battle failed to draw the attention of any other zombies and they made it through the rest of the intersection with no conflict. Most of Fourth was littered with the wreckage of cars and undead, so they made their way over to Fifth, which was more of the same.

They skirted round the back of Independence Hall and decided to stick to alleys and side streets as the traffic there was minimal. They were passing the Philadelphia Parking Authority when all hell broke loose.

The lights on Filbert Street were dark, pitching the entire block into an eerie and still gloom. They trod warily down the street then a car alarm split the silence of the night to their left. A zombie thrashed inside the car, its fists beating a staccato on the passenger side window. The blaring sound was a beacon to hundreds of zombies who stood idly in the Parking Authority. All at once, like a river bursting through a dam, the horde of zombies rushed into the street. The three punks were immediately surrounded.

Razzle raised his iron pipe like William Wallace in <u>Braveheart</u> and shouted, "If we're dying here tonight, we're going out in style!"

He yanked the headphone cord out of the Walkman, turned the dial all the way up and hit PLAY There was silence for three seconds in which only the grunting and shuffling of the army of zombies could be heard. They closed around the three punks, who stood back to back with their makeshift weapons raised. Then, the distorted sound of "Astro Zombies" by the Misfits blared out of the personal cassette player.

The song shrieked for ten seconds until Glenn Danzig's tortured voice came over the speaker. The zombies closest to the punks stopped. In unison, they threw back their heads and howled. This quickly spread throughout the mob and within moments, hundreds of zombies wailed into the night sky.

When the second verse started, a woman dressed as Catwoman, standing near the punks, went silent. She stood with her mouth open as black ooze seeped from her eyes, nose and ears. Her head shook for a moment and then exploded. Black slush erupted from her neck and pattered down like toxic rain.

Within seconds, more heads exploded, slicking the road with blackened jelly. The punks stood in awe at the gruesome scene. Less than two minutes later, as Danzig yelled out the word "Go", the entire zombie horde laid headless in a circle on Filbert Street, as if dark magic radiated out from the trio of punks.

***

They walked the rest of the way to the Trocadero with the mix tape turned all the way up. Any zombies that came within earshot performed the same bizarre ritual. Razzle switched songs from the UK Subs to the X-Ray Spex to Propaghandi and they all had the same effect. Once safely inside the fortified theater, he told the other survivors about their super-weapon. By the next morning, the word had spread throughout the punk and hardcore scene.

Across the country, punk rock was played thousands of times and the zombie apocalypse was averted.

A memorial wall was built on Penn's Landing, commemorating the lives lost that day. The first name to grace the wall was Holly Hell. Every Halloween, a small group of punks led by Razzle, Allison and Nat, all dressed to the nines in their faded leather, spiked Mohawks and Doc Marten's, met at the wall and sang a rowdy rendition of "Astro Zombies".

Meet the Authors

Ed Ahern resumed writing after forty odd years in foreign intelligence and international sales. He's had over three hundred stories and poems published so far, and six books. Ed works the other side of writing at Bewildering Stories, where he sits on the review board and manages a posse of six review editors.
https://www.twitter.com/bottomstripper

Olivia Arieti lives in Torre del Lago Puccini, Italy, with her family. She writes drama, poetry and fiction. Her stories have appeared in several magazines and anthologies including, *Enchanted Conversations, Enchanted Tales Literary Magazine, Fantasia Divinity Magazine, Forgotten Tomb Press, Horrified Press, Infective Ink, Pandemonium Press, Sirens Call Publications, Blood Song Books, Black Hare Press, Pussy Magic Magazine, Stormy Island Publishing, Breaking Rules Publishing, Scarlet Leaf Review, Iron Faerie Publishing, Dark Dossier Magazine, Paramour Ink Press, Raven and Drake Publishing.*

Diane Arrelle has more than 350 short stories published and two short story collections: Just A Drop In The Cup and Seasons On The Dark Side. She, her sane husband and insane cat live on the edge of the New Jersey (USA) Pine Barrens (home of the Jersey Devil).

Dorothy Davies is an editor, writer, photographer and medium. Somehow all these things come together in her seemingly crowded leisure and work life. She retired from editing for a while to run a second hand shop, the best one on the Isle of Wight, but the thrill of finding and publishing outstanding stories became too much so she started again with the Gravestone Press imprint. She has since closed the shop, here being other things to do… Her book, The Skullface Chronicles, the story of a zombie taking revenge on his dysfunctional family, is available through fiction4all.com. She has a box full of short stories, some of which are finding their way into the anthologies, having not seen daylight for many a long year. She also channels books from spirit authors, notable figures from our history. These can be found on the fiction4all.site under Zadkiel Publishing.

Paul Edwards is a life-long horror fan and writes his own twisted tales in any spare time that he can grab. He has seen three collections of stories published – Now That I've Lost You (Screaming Dreams), Black Mirrors (Rainfall Books) and Night Voices (Demain Publishing), the latter being a joint-collection with author Frank Duffy. Paul is also a fan of role-playing games, rock music and rough Somerset cider.

Jason R Frei lives in Eastern Pennsylvania where he works as a therapist with children and adolescents. He writes speculative fiction culled from the experiences of his life and those he works with and blends science fiction, fantasy and horror into new creations. His flash story "The Garden" will be featured in the horror anthology *99 Tiny Terrors* by Pulse Publishing and his short story "Some of the Parts" will be featured in the horror anthology *Toilet Zone 3: The Royal Flush* by Hellbound Books Publishing. Visit him online:

Geoff Nelder lives in Manchester with his physicist wife, cycling rural lanes for thinking time. Geoff is a former teacher, now an editor, writer and fiction competition judge. His novels include historical fantasy Vengeance Island; Scifi: Alien Exit; The ARIA trilogy; The vegan scifi Flying Crooked series with Suppose We released 2019 followed by Falling Up; Kepler's Son and Vanished Earth on the way. thrillers: Escaping Reality, and Hot Air.
Collection: Incremental– 25 surreal tales more mental than incremental. Non-fiction includes climate books relating to his urban microclimate research, winning him a Fellowship of the Royal Meteorological Society.
Geoff's website: https://geoffnelder.com

Rie Sheridan Rose multitasks. A lot. Her short stories appear in numerous anthologies, including Killing It Softly Vol. 1 & 2, Hides the Dark Tower, Dark Divinations and On Fire. She has authored twelve novels, six poetry chapbooks and lyrics for dozens of songs. She is also editor-in-chief for Mocha Memoirs Press and editor for the Thirteen O' Clock imprint of Horrified Press.

Rickey Rivers Jr was born and raised in Alabama. He is a Best of the Net nominated writer and cancer survivor. His work has appeared in the JJ Outre Review, Stellium Literary Magazine, Fabula Argentea (among other publications).

David Turnbull is a member of the Clockhouse London group of genre writers. He writes mainly short fiction and has had numerous short stories published in magazines and anthologies. His stories have previously been featured at Liars League London events and read at other live events such as Solstice Shorts and Virtual Futures. He was born in Scotland, but now lives in the Catford area of London. He can be found at www.tumsh.co.uk.

Liam A Spinage is a former philosophy student, former archaeology educator and former police clerk who spends most of his spare time on the beach gazing up at the sky and across the sea while his imagination runs riot.